BOOT-HILL SHOWDOWN

He was a strong man, in good condition, and used to hard work, so the grave went down swiftly.

He was less than halfway down when the riders began to come.

He slipped the thong from his six-shooter and continued to work.

There were three of them, all strangers. All the horses wore the Circle M brand of the Munsons.

The speaker was a wide-hipped, narrow-shouldered man with a narrow-brimmed hat.

"You diggin' that grave for one or two?" he asked.

BENDIGO SHAFTER
BORDEN CHANTRY
BOWDRIE
BOWDRIE'S LAW
BRIONNE
THE BROKEN GUN
BUCKSKIN RUN
THE BURNING HILLS
THE CALIFORNIOS
CALLAGHEN
CATLOW
CHANCY
THE CHEROKEE TRAIL
COMSTOCK LODE
CONAGHER
CROSSFIRE TRAIL
DARK CANYON
DOWN THE LONG HILLS
DUTCHMAN'S FLAT
THE EMPTY LAND
FAIR BLOWS THE WIND
FALLON
THE FERGUSON RIFLE
THE FIRST FAST DRAW
FLINT
FRONTIER
GUNS OF THE TIMBERLANDS
HANGING WOMAN CREEK
THE HAUNTED MESA
HELLER WITH A GUN
THE HIGH GRADERS
HIGH LONESOME
THE HILLS OF HOMICIDE
HONDO
HOW THE WEST WAS WON
THE IRON MARSHAL
THE KEY-LOCK MAN
KID RODELO
KILKENNY
KILLOE
KILRONE
KIOWA TRAIL
LAST STAND AT PAPAGO
  WELLS
LAW OF THE DESERT BORN
THE LONESOME GODS
THE MAN CALLED NOON
THE MAN FROM SKIBBEREEN
MATAGORDA
MILO TALON
THE MOUNTAIN VALLEY WAR
NIGHT OVER THE SOLOMONS
NORTH TO THE RAILS
OVER ON THE DRY SIDE
 PASSIN' THROUGH

THE PROVING TRAIL
THE QUICK AND THE DEAD
RADIGAN
REILLY'S LUCK
THE RIDER OF LOST CREEK
THE RIDER OF THE RUBY HILLS
RIDING FOR THE BRAND
RIVERS WEST
THE SHADOW RIDERS
SHALAKO
SHOWDOWN AT YELLOW
  BUTTE
SILVER CANYON
SITKA
SON OF A WANTED MAN
THE STRONG SHALL LIVE
TAGGART
TO TAME A LAND
TUCKER
UNDER THE SWEET-
  WATER RIM
UTAH BLAINE
THE WALKING DRUM
WAR PARTY
WESTWARD THE TIDE
WEST FROM SINGAPORE
WHERE THE LONG GRASS
  BLOWS
YONDERING

Sackett Titles by
Louis L'Amour

---

1. SACKETT'S LAND
2. TO THE FAR BLUE
   MOUNTAINS
3. THE DAYBREAKERS
4. SACKETT
5. LANDO
6. MOJAVE CROSSING
7. THE SACKETT BRAND
8. THE LONELY MEN
9. TREASURE MOUNTAIN
10. MUSTANG MAN
11. GALLOWAY
12. THE SKY-LINERS
13. THE MAN FROM THE
    BROKEN HILLS
14. RIDE THE DARK TRAIL
15. THE WARRIOR'S PATH
16. LONELY ON THE
    MOUNTAIN
17. RIDE THE RIVER
18. JUBAL SACKETT

MATAGORDA
LOUIS L'AMOUR

BANTAM BOOKS
TORONTO • NEW YORK • LONDON • SYDNEY • AUCKLAND

MATAGORDA

A Bantam Book / November 1967

2nd printing .. February 1968	4th printing ...... July 1969
3rd printing .... August 1968	5th printing .. February 1970
6th printing ... July 1970	

New Bantam edition / June 1971

2nd printing .. October 1971	13th printing ..... May 1978
3rd printing ..... May 1972	14th printing ..... July 1979
4th printing . November 1972	15th printing ..... April 1980
5th printing . September 1973	16th printing ..... May 1981
6th printing .. October 1973	17th printing ..... May 1981
7th printing . September 1974	18th printing ..... June 1982
8th printing . December 1974	19th printing ..... April 1983
9th printing ... January 1976	20th printing ... March 1984
10th printing ..... July 1976	21st printing .. February 1985
11th printing .. February 1977	22nd printing ..... May 1986
12th printing . September 1977	23rd printing .... March 1987
24th printing ... April 1988	

Photograph of Louis L'Amour
by John Hamilton—Globe Photos, Inc.

ISBN 0-553-25221-6

Published simultaneously in the United States and Canada

Bantam Books are published by Bantam Books, a division of
Bantam Doubleday Dell Publishing Group, Inc. Its trademark,
consisting of the words "Bantam Books" and the portrayal of
a rooster, is Registered in U.S. Patent and Trademark Office
and in other countries. Marca Registrada. Bantam Books,
666 Fifth Avenue, New York, New York 10103.

PRINTED IN THE UNITED STATES OF AMERICA

KR   33 32 31 30 29 28 27 26 25 24

MATAGORDA

1

Major Tappan Duvarney rested his hands on the rail and stared toward the low sandy shore. It was not what he had expected of Texas, but whatever lay ahead represented his last chance. He had to make it here or nowhere.

He listened to the rhythmic pound and splash of the paddle wheels and looked bleakly into the future. Behind him lay the War Between the States and several years of Indian fighting with the frontier army; before him only the lonely years at some sun-baked, windswept frontier post, with nothing to look forward to but retirement.

When the war had broken out he was a young man with an assured future. Aside from the family plantation in Virginia, his father owned a shipping line trading to the West Indies and Gulf ports—four schooners and a barkentine, and good vessels all.

Tap Duvarney had made two trips before the mast on the barkentine, had taken examinations for his ticket, and had made two trips as third mate, one aboard a schooner, the other on the barkentine. His father wanted him to know the sea and its business from every aspect, and Tap liked the sea. He had taken to the rough and rowdy life in Caribbean ports as if born to it.

The war changed all that. His sympathies and those of his family were with the Union. He had gone north and joined up. Renegades had burned the plantation buildings and run off the stock; one schooner had been lost in a hurricane off this very coast, two others had been confiscated by the Confederacy and sunk by Union gunboats. The barkentine had disappeared into that mysterious triangle south of Bermuda and left nothing behind but the memory. The last schooner, beat and bedraggled, had burned alongside the dock when the war came to Charleston. Tap Duvarney returned from the war saddled with debts, his father dead, his home destroyed.

There seemed only one thing to do, and he did it. He went back to the army and a series of frontier posts. During the nine years following the war he fought Indians from the Dakotas to Arizona. He managed to keep his hair, but picked up three scars, one from a knife, two from bullet wounds.

Finally, his father's estate had been settled and he emerged from the shambles with a bit more than seven thousand dollars.

It was then he heard from Tom Kittery.

Captain Wilkes stopped beside him now on his way to the pilot house. Duvarney knew that Wilkes was worried about him, and genuinely wished to help. The captain was a good man who had served on one of his father's ships.

"You'll find Texas a fast country, Major. Do you have friends here?"

"One . . . so far as I know. I met him during the war."

"You haven't seen him since? That's quite a while,

Major. Is that the man you've gone into partnership with?"

Duvarney thought he detected a doubtful note in Wilkes's voice, and he was not surprised. He was a bit doubtful himself from time to time.

"I know the man, Captain. Whatever else he may be, he's honest . . . and he's got guts. I go along with that."

"The cattle business is good," Wilkes said. "Indianola has been the biggest cattle-shipping port in Texas for a good long time, so I've had a good deal to do with it. I may know your partner."

"Kittery . . . Tom Kittery. Old Texas family."

"Kittery, is it? Yes, he has guts, all right. There isn't a man in Texas would deny that. And he's honest. But speaking as a friend, I'd never leave the ship, if I were you. Come on back to New Orleans. You're a good man, and you know the sea. We'll find something for you there."

"What's wrong with Kittery?"

"With *him?* Nothing . . . nothing at all." Wilkes glanced at Duvarney. "I take it you haven't heard about the feud?"

Wilkes paused, then went on. "You're walking right into the middle of a shooting war . . . the Munson-Kittery feud. It has been going on since 1840 or thereabouts, and from the moment it is discovered that you are associated with Kittery you'll be a prime target."

"I know nothing about any feud."

"You say you knew Kittery during the war? He may have thought the feud was a thing of the past because it seemed to be over. Until the Kittery boys left for the war there hadn't been any shooting for several years.

"In the years before the war the Kittery faction numbered some of the toughest, ablest fighting men in Texas; so the Munsons laid low and played their music soft. And when the Kittery boys went off to war, the Munsons stayed home.

"Even so, they kept quiet until Ben was killed at

Shiloh. That started them stirring around a bit, but it wasn't until Tom was captured—reported dead, in fact —that they began to cut loose.

"They ran off a bunch of Kittery cattle, then burned a barn. Old Alec, Tom's uncle, rode out after the Munsons and they ambushed him and killed him. After that they really cut loose. They killed two Negro hands who had worked for the Kitterys for years, and burned the old home—one of the oldest houses on the coast.

"Cattle were beginning to be worth money, and the Munsons thought they were rich on Kittery beef. Only somebody stampeded the biggest herd one night and ran them into the Big Thicket. Well, you don't know the Thicket, but finding cattle in there is like hunting ghosts. The Munsons never were much on hard work, and rousting those steers from the Thicket would be the hardest kind of work. So the steers, and a lot of other cattle, are still in there."

"Maybe those are the cattle I bought," Duvarney commented ironically. "It's my luck."

"Are you wearing a gun?" Wilkes asked.

"I have one." As a matter of fact, he had two guns. "From what you've said, I should be wearing one."

"You should." Wilkes straightened up. "I'm going up to take her in, but my advice to you is: stay on the ship. . . . If you do leave her, be ready for trouble. They laid for Johnny Lubec, and they laid for Tom. They were waiting for him when the boat docked . . . my boat."

"Tom?"

Wilkes smiled grimly. "Tom was no fool. I told him what had happened to Johnny, so he left the ship as we were going past the island, entering the bay.

"The fog was thick that morning, and he lowered himself over the side on a raft we'd built for him, and paddled ashore. He slipped ashore on Matagorda Island, and nobody knows the island better than Tom. It's long, but so narrow you wouldn't think a man could hide there, but he managed it. Anyway, he was still alive the last time we were here, and I hope he still is."

"You mentioned Johnny Something-or-other?"

"Lubec. Johnny wasn't a Kittery, just an orphan kid they took in and treated like one of the family. Folks said that Johnny's pa was one of the Jean Lafitte pirates . . . they had a hide-out on Matagorda themselves and used to careen their ships on the landward beaches.

"Anyway, Johnny grew up with the Kitterys, so when he came home the Munsons were laying for him. They shot him down and left him for dead, then went off to have a drink, and Johnny crawled away. He got to the house of an old Indian who lives on Black Jack Point, and the Indian cared for him.

"The Munsons were fit to be tied when Tom gave them the slip. If they'd known Tom was alive they would never have reopened the fight, not even with Jackson Huddy or the Harts around to help. At that, they almost got Tom."

"What happened?"

"Tom rode over to his old home. Nobody had told him the place was burned out, and I guess he figured some of his people might be there. He rode home and the Munsons were laying for him. They heard him coming and shot him out of the saddle, put two bullets into him.

"Jim Hart and two renegade riders of the Munson crowd were there, and when Tom fell they just knew they had him. They ran in on him and he killed one of them and burned Hart a couple of times. Then he crawled to his horse, pulled himself into the saddle, and rode off.

"Tom must have figured he was dying, or he wouldn't have done what he did. He rode to the Munson place and hollered up the folks. Well, they'd no idea Tom was even alive. Word hadn't got back from Indianola yet, so old Taylor Munson, the bull of the woods, came to the door. Tom told him who he was, and shot him down. And then Tom dropped from sight."

Tap Duvarney stared gloomily toward the nearing shore. He had bought a partnership in a herd of cattle to be driven to Kansas . . . not a feud. He wanted no part of it.

"Months went by," Wilkes went on, "and nobody saw hide nor hair of Tom. The Munsons hunted him high and low, and finally they were ready to believe he was dead. Cattle had become big business, so the Munsons rounded up a herd and started for Kansas. When they were close to Doan's Store, Dale Munson rode over to pick up the mail and some tobacco, and ran right into Tom Kittery.

"First any of the Munson crowd knew of it was when Dale's horse came into camp with Dale tied over the saddle. There were two bullet holes in Dale's chest you could cover with a silver dollar."

"You mentioned a Jackson Huddy," Duvarney said.

"He's a killer. Some say he's kin to the Munsons. Anyway, he runs with them, and after old Taylor Munson was killed Huddy sort of moved into command. And I mean it is a command.

"When it looked like the fight was going their way, Munsons began showing up from all over. I'd say there were forty or more gun-packing men in the clan. And they've played it smart. Two of their kin are elected to office, a sheriff and a judge. Another one is a deputy over to Victoria."

When Wilkes had finished speaking he went to the pilot house, and Tappan Duvarney lingered by the rail.

He had no choice, he was thinking. Every cent he owned beyond what he carried in his money belt— and that was little enough—was invested with Tom Kittery, who was supposed to be buying cattle and hiring an outfit.

It was an odd friendship that had developed between the two men. Tap Duvarney, then a lowly lieutenant in the Union forces, had been sent south on a secret mission. His southern accent was perfect for it, as was his knowledge of the country. Trouble developed when he ran into Captain Tom Kittery. He captured Tom, but he was more than a hundred miles from the nearest Union outpost.

He had a choice of turning Tom loose, which would mean his own pursuit and capture, shooting him in cold blood, or trying to take him back. Tap Duvarney decided on the last.

On the way, although Tom was continually trying to outwit Tap and escape, the two developed a respect and a liking for each other. During the long hours en route, Tom talked a good deal of Texas and the cattle business, suggesting that if they came out of the war alive they should become partners. And that had been the beginning of it.

Walking back to his cabin now, Tap Duvarney dug down into his sea chest and got out a Russian .44 Smith & Wesson. The holster was worn from use, but he belted it on. He hesitated a bit over the second pistol, then thrust it into his waistband.

Pausing before the mirror, he straightened his cravat, and studied the hang on his coat to see if the pistol showed a bulge. It did not.

For a moment then, he looked at himself.

What he saw was a lean, spare-built man with a brown, quiet face and hazel eyes. His shoulders were broad, and the coat fitted admirably. He was, he thought wryly, what he had heard people say of him: "a handsome man," or "a fine figure of a man." He was also a man of thirty-three with a wealth of experience, and nothing to show for it but the scars. When most men of his age were well established in their life work, he had nothing, was nothing.

He had found it all too easy to slip into the routine of army life, but the peacetime army offered little chance for advancement, and he had been lucky to make major. He knew of many older men who had done just as much who were captains, and a few who were still lieutenants. But his early life had been geared to ambition, and he felt he must accomplish something, do something, make himself a better man, and his country a better place. This he had been taught as a child, this he still believed.

He turned from the mirror, gathered up his gear, and swung his sea chest to his shoulder with practiced ease. Then he picked up the carpetbag and walked out on deck, placing his things near the gangway.

Several passengers had come out on deck to watch the steamboat's approach to Indianola. Most of them he knew by sight, and had measured and catalogued them. All except two fell into familiar categories. One of these was a tall, wiry man in a tailored black broadcloth suit, a hawk-faced man with a saturnine expression, as if he viewed the world with wry amusement. The other was a girl.

She was young, and beautiful in the way a ranch girl is beautiful who does not know the skills or artifices of the city. She was blonde, with blue eyes and a clear, fresh complexion, but she looked somewhat sullen now, and seemed to be approaching the Texas coast with no anticipation of pleasure.

Several times Duvarney had caught her eyes upon him, showing curiosity but nothing more. He lifted his hat. "Ma'am, I presume you are acquainted in Indianola?"

"Yes, I am," she answered. "My home is in Texas."

"A fine state, I've heard. I was wondering if you could tell me where I could locate Tom Kittery."

Her eyes were suddenly unfriendly. She looked at him, a hard, measuring glance. "If you are looking for Tom Kittery you will have to find him yourself. If there is anyone who knows where he is, I don't know about it."

"I see. Well, no harm done. I expect he will find me soon enough, when he knows I am here. He has enemies, I believe?"

"He has . . . too many of them."

Then they stood silently together, watching the approaching shore, and Tap found himself wondering about her. She was dressed neatly but not expensively, in the style of a ranch girl going to the city, or coming back from a visit. From her attitude, she was not happy about coming home.

"You enjoyed New Orleans, ma'am?"

She turned quickly. "Oh, I did! It's a wonderful place, so many people, beautiful clothes . . . so many nice places to go—if there was somebody to take you."

"You have friends there?"

"I have an uncle and aunt there. I'm afraid they did not approve of a lot of the most exciting places."

"Quite properly," Duvarney commented dryly. "The most interesting places in New Orleans are no place for a young girl.

"As for me," he added, "I look forward to Indianola, and to Texas."

"You're going to *stay* there?"

"I hope to. As a matter of fact, I have some investments there. An investment, I should say. In cattle."

She looked at him. "You did not mention your name. Or where you were from."

"Sorry, ma'am. The name is Tappan Duvarney, and I am from Virginia."

"*You're* Tap Duvarney?"

He was surprised. "You've heard of me, then?"

"I'm Mady Coppinger." She glanced quickly around to be sure no one else was listening. "Tom Kittery is my . . . he is a friend of mine. He told me about you. As a matter of fact," she added, somewhat irritably, "he has been talking of very little else since you decided to come down."

She looked hard at him again. "Tom said you'd lived in Richmond and Charleston."

"A long time ago. For years I've only visited there. I've been in the army . . . out west."

"I envy you. Any place is better than Texas." The

sullen look was on her face once more. "I wish I had never come back. I hate it."

"Do you go to New Orleans often."

"I've never been there before, and it isn't likely I'll get to go again." She looked suddenly defiant. "Unless somebody takes me."

He avoided the opening, if that was what it was, and watched the shore. He could see the buildings now. The coast was low and flat, but there seemed to be hills beyond the town which were vague at that distance. The two long dark fingers of pier thrust into the bay waters.

"I've never been anywhere before," the girl said. "Only to Indianola or Victoria . . . and once over to Beeville. My pa owns a ranch."

"Does he live near Tom?"

She shook her head. "Mr. Duvarney, you must understand something. Tom Kittery is a hunted man. The Munsons are looking for him and when they find him they'll kill him. If you want to stay alive, don't you dare mention his name, or they'll be gunning for you."

"I will have to find Tom."

"Don't you go asking for him. I'd say you'd best hire yourself a rig . . . or a horse." She looked up at him. "Do you ride?"

"I was in the cavalry."

"Then get a horse and ride south. Take your time. Ride south toward Mission River. If nobody stops you keep on riding, but don't be in a hurry. Tom will find you."

"It doesn't seem a very good time to gather a herd for a cattle drive," Duvarney commented.

"Tom usually does what he starts out to do," Mady said. "I'll have to say that. Like the business with the hides."

At his questioning look, she went on. "The Munsons have been branding Rafter K stock. The Rafter K is the Kittery brand, but the law is a Munson and there wasn't much Tom could do, or so folks thought. Then one morning they woke up and found fresh hides tacked up where everybody could see them. They were nailed up with the hair side against the wall so any western man could see the Rafter K had been changed into a Munson Circle M."

She smiled, and suddenly her face was changed. "Everybody in the country was laughing about that, and telling the story, until Jim Hart killed a man over to Beeville. Since then nobody feels much like talking, but the hides are still going up. Tom has nailed up hides in Beeville, Indianola, and Victoria, and even clean down to Brownsville. The Munsons are mad enough to eat nails."

Tap chuckled. "No wonder they're mad." He straightened up. "How about you? Do they know you're a friend of his?"

"They know it. But mister, nobody bothers a woman in Texas. They may not like me, but they won't do anything or say anything. Even if they weren't afraid of Texas people, they wouldn't say anything because of Jackson Huddy."

"But I thought he was one of them?"

"He is. Jackson Huddy is probably the quickest man alive with a gun . . . quicker than Tom, some think. But whatever else he is—and he has the name of being the coldest killer this country ever saw—he respects a woman. He respects women and the church, and very little else. You look out for him."

Duvarney tipped his hat and moved away from her. It would never do to invite trouble for her by staying near her. The possibility that they knew about him was slight, yet somehow they had known that Johnny Lubec and Tom were coming home, and they had been waiting for them. Somehow they might also know about him.

He stood by the gangway and watched the lines go out, and then the gangway. Captain Wilkes came down from the pilot house to bid his passengers good-bye. One by one he saw them down the gangway and onto the pier.

Several rigs were waiting there, and in turn they drove away with passengers and their luggage. Only one remained behind.

Warily, Tap Duvarney studied the men on the dock. There was the usual collection of loafers who gathered to see any boat or train arrive. But there were three who drew more than his casual attention. He had lived too long on the frontier not to know trouble-hunters when he saw them, and two of these seemed to be in that category. The third man was a tall, high-shouldered man with a clean-shaven, hard-boned face and small eyes. Once, briefly, his eyes met Duvarney's.

The others on the dock were familiar types. In most towns there are men or boys who want to try their strength, usually against somebody they feel confident they can whip. Often the man they choose is a stranger —if a well-dressed stranger, so much the better. Such men he did not mind, for they started their fights and they took their medicine, learning their lesson as all must do.

But there was another kind, the real bullies, those with a drive to meanness and sadism. These three, he felt sure, were of that sort. He had been the butt of the joke before, knew the dialogue, and was ready.

Only he had not wanted it to happen here, when he had just arrived in the town where Tom Kittery had enemies. A fight he would not mind, and might even welcome as a way to initiate himself into the local scene, but he did not want a bullet in the back because of it.

When the last of the passengers had gone, he lifted his sea chest to his left shoulder, then picked up his carpetbag with his right hand, following the last man by a few steps.

The buckboard with the two paint mustangs was still standing at the end of the pier. If the driver was around, he was not in sight.

Duvarney walked along to the end of the pier and

put down his sea chest and carpetbag near the buck-board. He glanced around, hearing the boots of the two young men as they came up behind him. He turned slowly when they were still several feet off.

They had moved apart a little, so he waited, some-what bored by the familiarity of the pattern. "You fixin' to ask that man for a ride, mister?" one of them asked.

"I might at that. Is he around?"

"Name of Foster. Got a way of comin' an' goin', Foster has. He might be around, and he might not. Thing is, have you got any right to be here? Seems to me a man comin' to a strange town should have some money, and if he has money he should stand up for the drinks."

"That's fair enough. You boys carry my trunk up to the hotel and I'll buy you each a drink."

"Carry your— What do you think we are, mister? Beggars?"

"No," he said, "only I figured you could earn money enough for a bath and a shave. Might seem nice to be clean again . . . after so long a time."

They stared at him, then the taller one took a step nearer. "You tryin' to be smart, mister? You sayin' we're dirty?"

Duvarney widened his eyes. "I wouldn't think of such a thing. I'm not a man who stresses the obvious. I just offered you a chance to earn the drink you asked for."

"We never asked for no drink," the tall one argued. "We figured a gent like you, so dressed up an' all, we just figured you might have money enough to treat the boys up yonder. Suppose you let us see how much you got."

"Sorry. If you intend to rob me, you'll have to try it the hard way."

Duvarney stepped back, as the tall one started for him, but as he stepped back he kicked the carpetbag into the other's path, tripping the young man so that he fell to hands and knees. As Duvarney kicked the carpetbag, he shifted his feet and met the lunge of the second man.

He was coming in low, and Tap jerked his knee up hard into the man's face, smashing nose and lips. Catching him by the hair, he jerked him upright and swung a right into his belly. The man went down hard as Tap wheeled and caught a wild right on the shoulder from the first man, now on his feet. Tap looked at him and laughed, then he feinted and the man's hands flailed wildly. Tap stabbed a left to the mouth, then three more as fast as he could jab. He feinted again, hitting him in the wind, and when he bent over gasping, a hammer blow on the kidney stretched him out.

Calmly, Duvarney straightened his coat. Captain Wilkes was standing by the rail of the steamboat, watching. The tall, lean man who had apparently been with the two he had just beaten, looked on without emotion, or evidence of more than casual interest.

"That there was mighty neat," he said. "Looks to me like you've fought some with your fists."

"A little."

The man gestured toward the two on the dock, who were groaning now, and beginning to stir. "Don't let that set you up none. They never was much account." He started to turn away toward town, then paused. "If you're huntin' the man who owns that rig, you'll find him yonder. You can tell any who ask that he just kept the wrong company."

"How does a man choose his company around here?"

The tall man looked at Duvarney with cool, almost uninterested eyes. "He chooses any company he likes, just so it ain't Kitterys. We don't cotton to Kitterys."

"Afraid of them?"

The man looked at him. "I am Jackson Huddy," he said, and walked away up the street.

2

Duvarney watched Jackson Huddy walk slowly away and his eyes went beyond him to the weather-beaten frame buildings, the signs hanging out over the streets, the hitching rails. It looked not at all like a port on the Gulf of Mexico, but rather like a cow town in the Plains country or the Rockies.

The two roughnecks were getting up. One, whose face had had a hard encounter with Tap's knee, had a badly broken nose, by the look of it; the swelling had already almost closed his eyes, and his lips were a pulp.

Neither of them had known anything about fist-fighting. As for Duvarney, he had served a harsh apprenticeship when he made those two trips to the West Indies as a deck hand, to say nothing of two trips as a mate. In those days no man could hold down a job aft unless he could fight. He was expected to be ready and able to whip any man in the crew, and any three if necessary.

Duvarney stood watching the two, but as they got up they backed off. He was wary of a shot in the back, but neither man seemed to remember that he carried a gun.

When they had gone he glanced reluctantly at the stack of cotton bales toward which Jackson Huddy had gestured.

With another glance up the street, Duvarney walked over to the bales. A man lay behind the pile, sprawled on his face, and there was blood in the dust where he rested.

Duvarney turned him over. The man had been stabbed twice in the belly, the long blade striking upward. He was dead, the body not yet cold. On his holster was burned a Rafter K, the brand of the Kitterys.

Returning to the buckboard, Duvarney made a space in the back for the body, then brought it over and laid it out in the back, covering it with an old tarp that lay there.

In the buckboard was a nose bag for the horse and a sack of oats, as well as two sacks of groceries. He saw that the mustangs also carried the Rafter K brand.

He stepped up to the seat and turned the buckboard around. He drove up the street, aware of the eyes that followed him. He drove to a sign that said Hardware, got down, and went inside. A small group congregated around the buckboard, and more than one of them lifted the tarp to look at the dead man.

"Is there an undertaker in town?" Duvarney asked.

The gray-haired man behind the counter shook his head. "Nobody will lay out a Kittery man," he said "and Foster was a Kittery man. And there ain't nobody will dig a grave for him, either. Nor pray for him."

"It's that kind of town?"

The man shrugged. "We live here, mister. We live here all the time, and that Munson crowd are here. I'm sorry, right sorry."

"Is there a Kittery lot in the cemetery?"

"Two . . . maybe three of them."

"I'll need a pick and a shovel."

"You'll need more than that, mister. You'll need a rifle."

"All right, hand me down one of those Winchesters, and I'll want about five hundred rounds of ammunition."

"*Five hundred* rounds? That would fight a small war."

"You can pass the word for me that I have no part in this feud, and I want no part in it; but if they ask for any kind of trouble they can have it.

"You can also pass the word around that I am going to bury this man, and that I am asking for no help. I will read over him myself."

The storekeeper was silent, putting the order together swiftly. When Duvarney paid him, he said, "Don't think we're unfeeling. This fight has been going on for nearly forty years now, and a lot of good men have been killed. Nobody wants to get involved any more. It's their fight, so let them have it."

"All I want to do is bury a man."

"You won't do it. They won't let you."

The crowd moved back for him when he put the pick and shovel into the wagon beside the body. They stood back even further when he loaded the ammunition and a few items in the way of food. Then he got up on the buckboard and spoke to the team. They started with a rush.

At the cemetery he drove the buckboard through the gate and closed it after him. He scouted among the graves until he found the Kittery lot; then he peeled off his coat, which he put over a tombstone beside him, one of his guns hidden beneath it. The other he left in its holster. The Winchester he leaned out of sight near the buckboard. Then he went to work.

He worked swiftly down through the top soil for a good two feet. Then it became slower work, but he kept on. He was a strong man, in good condition, and used to hard work, but he realized that he would be lucky to finish before dark. He had the grave less than half dug when the riders began to come. He slipped the thong from his six-shooter and continued to dig.

There were three of them. All the horses wore the Circle M brand of the Munsons. Within a few minutes there were four more, then others, some of these hanging back, obviously come to see the fun.

"You diggin' that grave for one or two?"

Duvarney ignored it, managed three more spadefuls of dirt before the question came again. He straightened up, leaned on his shovel, and looked at them. He was waist-deep in the hole with a parapet of dirt thrown up in front of him. Three large tombstones formed almost a wall along his route to the buckboard.

"I asked was you diggin' that for one, or two?"

The speaker was a wide-hipped, narrow-shouldered man with a narrow-brimmed hat.

"For one," Duvarney replied. "You'll have to dig your own, if you want one."

Somebody among the spectators snickered, and the man turned sharply around. The snickering stopped.

"When you get that grave deep enough, you'll find out who it's for. We aim to bury you right there."

Jackson Huddy had ridden up, and he was watching and listening. Duvarney leaned on the shovel. "You boys aren't very smart," he said. "I've got a lot more cover than you. I figure to get three or four before you get me . . . if you ever do."

For a moment that stopped them. He had only to drop to his knees to leave only head and shoulders in view. There was no cover for them outside the fence, and a man at that range should do pretty well. Nobody spoke, and Duvarney resumed his digging.

Suddenly the man with the narrow-brimmed hat started to crawl through the fence.

"Shab," Huddy was saying, "you come back here. That man is buryin' the dead. There'll be no botherin' him. Anyway, he ain't a Kittery."

"That's a Kittery man he's buryin'!"

"Leave him be. I like a man with nerve."

There was no more talk, but nobody walked away.

Slowly, Duvarney completed his digging; then he wrapped the body in the tarpaulin and placed it in the bottom of the grave. He filled in the grave, while the men stood quietly. After that he went to the buckboard for his carpetbag and took out a Bible. He removed his hat, and began to read, and when he had finished the funeral text he had chosen, he sang *Rock of Ages*.

His voice was fairly good, and he managed to sing it well. Here and there a voice joined in. When he had finished the hymn he picked up his tools and went back to the buckboard, then returned for his coat. As he lifted it his right hand gripped the six-shooter. He brought it up, and walked back to the buckboard and placed the coat and the pistol on the seat. As he started to get up he lifted the rifle from where it had been hidden and with an easy motion swung to the seat.

He gathered the reins with his left hand, his right holding the Winchester. He drove to the gate, and when he reached it he pointed the Winchester at the nearest man, smiling as he did so. "Friend, I'd be pleased if you'd open the gate for me."

The man hesitated for a moment, then he walked over and opened the gate, standing back with it until Tap Duvarney had driven through.

"Thank you," Duvarney said. "Thank you very much." He glanced at Huddy, still sitting his horse, and regarding Duvarney with an enigmatic expression. "And thank you, Mr. Huddy. It hurts no man to respect the dead."

He spoke to the team and they moved forward down the road, but at the point where the road to the cemetery reached the main trail he turned sharply and took the trail south from town.

There was no sound behind him, but he did not turn his head to look back. He had a straight quarter of a mile before there was any cover, and despite the bouncing the buckboard was giving him, he could be hit by a good shot. He held the good pace at which they had started, wanting as much distance as he could get. He had no doubt he would be followed, and a buckboard leaves a definite trail.

When he had two miles behind him he drew up, and with a wry grin he loaded the rifle. "You damn fool," he muttered. "Forgetting a thing like that can get you killed.'"

The sun was down, the breeze cool off the Gulf, which lay some distance off on his left, beyond Powderhorn Lake, close by. He had a good memory for maps and charts, as a result of both his early training at sea and his years in the army. To go south he must first go inland, find the Green Lake road, and let it take him past the head of San Antonio Bay. Beyond that there stretched a wide piece of country, but between here and there he knew of no place to hide.

The twin tracks of the trail were plain enough, even at night, so he pushed on. The paint mustangs seemed to be glad to be moving and he held them to a good trot, which seemed to be the pace they liked. From time to time he drew up to listen for sounds of pursuit.

He was under no delusions about Jackson Huddy. Whatever else he might be, the man had a code of ethics of his own, and only that had prevented a bloody gun battle in the cemetery. He was sure that under other circumstances Huddy would never hesitate to kill him . . . if he could.

He had studied the charts in Wilkes's wheelhouse and had a fair understanding of the country, so after a while he took a chance and left the trail, cutting across toward Green Lake. By day they would find his tracks, of course, but by then he hoped to be far away.

Several times he drew up to give the mustangs a brief rest, but they seemed tireless and impatient to keep going. Give them their heads, he thought, and likely they'll take me right where I want to go.

It was well past midnight when he saw the shine of water on his right. That would be Green Lake. The mustangs were tired now, trotting only when they started down a slight grade . . . which was rare enough. But they had held the pace well.

The last miles before daylight were weary ones, but he kept the team moving until they reached the breaks of the Guadalupe.

The sky was gray with morning when he turned off into the trees and found a hollow screened from the trail. Here he unhitched the team and led them to water, and after that he picketed them on a patch of good grass not far from the buckboard. Then, a gun at hand, he drew a blanket over him and went to sleep.

It was high noon when the sun woke him, shining through the leaves of a cottonwood tree. For a minute or two he lay perfectly still, listening. Then he sat up.

The horses were not twenty yards off, heads up, ears pricked.

Duvarney came up off the ground like a cat, thrust his six-shooter into his belt, and reached for his gun belt and his other pistol. As he belted it on, he listened. The horses were looking back the way he had come.

He got the team and brought them back. Not wanting the jingle of trace chains to warn anyone of his presence, he tied them to the buckboard. Taking his rifle, he worked his way through the trees and brush to a place where he could watch the tracks he must have left.

He recognized the girl before he could make out any of her features. It was Mady Coppinger.

She was riding in a buckboard driven by a stalwart Negro. Two riders followed close behind. As they drew nearer he could see that the Negro's features looked more like those of an Indian. He was a lean, intelligent-looking man with watchful eyes.

He drew up as he neared the place where Duvarney had turned off. "I'm thinkin', ma'am, that he wouldn't have gone no further than this. That team will be plumb wore out by now. You want I should find him?"

"No. . . ." She hesitated, then turned to one of the

riders following. "Harry, do you think Huddy will follow him?"

"Huddy? No. He won't foller, but Shabbit will. Shabbit and those boys Duvarney whupped down to the dock. They'll be after his scalp, an' you can bet on it. Huddy won't do anything until Duvarney declares himself."

"We should find him and warn him."

Tap Duvarney made no move to leave the shelter of the brush. He did not know these men, and although they seemed to be riders from the Coppinger outfit, he did not want to chance it. His attention was on the girl. Mady was lovely, no question about it, and the figure that filled out the dress she wore was something to think about . . . or for Tom Kittery to think about. She was his girl.

Besides, Tap had a girl. Or he had one when he left Virginia.

The Negro spoke. "Ma'am, I think it best we leave him alone. I've been watching his trail, and he's a cautious man. The way I see it, going into the brush to hunt for him might prove a chancey thing."

"Caddo's right," Harry agreed.

Caddo spoke to the horses and they moved out. Harry turned slightly in his saddle and glanced back at the pecan tree under which Duvarney was crouched. Had something given him away? Some bird, or perhaps a squirrel? Some movement he had not seen or felt?

When their dust had settled he harnessed the horses and emerged from the copse where he had been hiding. At the point where he went back on the trail he got down and wiped out the tracks as best he could, then drove on. An Apache would have read the sign without slowing his pace, but these men might not be as good at reading sign.

The air was fresh and clean, and the mustangs, rested after their morning grazing and rest, were prepared to go. They were tough, wild stock, bred to the plains, and only half-broken. Duvarney drove on with only an occasional backward glance, holding to the trail followed by Mady Coppinger.

Somewhere to the south he would find Tom Kittery and whatever was left of his seven thousand dollars. He had already made up his mind about that. He would take whatever money was left and ride out, writing off the rest of it as a bad investment.

He had no part in the Kittery-Munson feud, and he wanted none. No mention had been made of it when they had discussed the buying of cattle for a drive north.

Having no knowledge of exactly where Tom Kittery might be, Duvarney decided just to drift south, scouting the country as he went. He had supplies and ammunition enough, and the terrain was easy for buckboard travel, being generally level or somewhat rolling, with good grass and clumps of trees. Along the rivers there were oaks and pecans, as well as dogwood, willow, and redbud.

Taking a dim trail, Tap drove down toward Blackjack Point, following the shore of the peninsula whenever possible. On the third day after seeing Mady Coppinger, he was camped near some low brush within sight of the sea. He had made a small fire of driftwood and was brewing coffee when he heard a rustle behind him.

He reached for the coffeepot with his left hand, drew his six-shooter with his right. Moving the coffee a little nearer the coals, he straightened up, then took a quick step back to his left, which put him into the deep shadow of a pecan tree, gun ready.

There was a chuckle from the brush, and Tom Kittery stepped out, followed by two other men. "See? I told you," Kittery said. "Ain't no catchin' him off-guard. I never knew such a skittish hombre."

Tom Kittery looked good, but he was thin. He was honed down by hiding out, worn by constant watching, but humor glinted from his eyes as he stepped forward, hand thrust out in greeting.

3

"Man, you are a sight to behold! Look at him, boys. This here's the on'y man ever took me. Captured me alive an' on the hoof, and I'd never believed it could be done! And then he smuggled me right by some renegades that would have strung me up like a horse thief for bein' a Johnny Reb. And him a Yank!"

"Hello, Tom," Tap said. "It's been a while."

Kittery grinned at him. There was genuine welcome in his eyes, and his hand clasp was firm and strong. "I've thought of you a good bit, Tap. I surely have."

"Have we got a herd?"

Some of the smile left Kittery's face. "Sort of. I've got to talk to you about that." He turned. "Tap Duvarney, this here's Johnny Lubec. And that's the Cajun ... a good man, right out of the Louisiana swamps."

Lubec was a small, wiry man, scarcely more than a boy, but a boy with old eyes, a boy who had seen trouble. The Cajun was tall, thin, angular, sallow of face, with dark, lank hair and a gold earring in each ear.

"What about the cattle?" Tap asked. "That was every cent I had in the world, Tom. I gambled on you."

"And you won't regret it, Tap. I've had troubles— I suppose you've heard about that?"

"I heard about it."

"When we talked I thought the feud was a thing of the past. It was just a matter of rounding up some of Dad's cattle. I didn't have any money, so with your money, our cattle and know-how, we could drive to Kansas and make some money. That's what I planned. The trouble was, the cattle had been stolen. Most of them, at least."

"So the drive is off?"

"Not on your tintype! We're rounding up cattle now. Fact is, we've got a good part of a herd stashed away. But that's a small part of it. Somehow we've got to slip three thousand head of cattle out of the country without the Munsons gettin' wind of it."

They walked back and sat down around the fire, and the Cajun disappeared into the darkness. "He'll keep watch, so don't you worry none. He's one of the very best."

"I met Mady Coppinger on the boat."

Tom Kittery shot him a quick glance. "Came back did she? I wouldn't have bet on it."

"I thought you two had an understanding."

Tom shrugged. "We have, sort of. Mady's fed up with Texas, fed up with dust, cows, bronc riders, and cookin' for ranch hands. She fell heir to a stack of Godey's Lady's Books, and since then all she does is pine. I keep tellin' her I ain't no city man, but she won't listen."

With another glance at Duvarney, he said, "How'd she look?"

"Great. She's a very pretty young woman."

Tom filled two cups with the hot coffee. "Did you see any Munsons? I mean, around Indianola."

Tap ignored the question. "How did you know I'd arrived? Or did you know?"

"Cap'n Wilkes. He dipped the flag when he passed the point. We'd agreed on the signal." He paused a moment. "You're drivin' the rig . . . where's Foster?"

"They killed him. He was killed just about the time we were coming up to the wharf. I buried him in your family lot."

"You *what?*"

"You didn't want him buried there? Didn't seem that I had much choice."

"They let you bury him? Of course, we'd want him in our lot, or anywhere we could manage, and the best. But Indianola is mostly a Munson town. There's two or three of the clan live there, and always some of them are circulatin' about."

Over coffee, Tap Duvarney told about the burial and the brief encounter with Shab, or Shabbit. Of the brief fight on the wharf he said nothing at all.

"Tom," he said abruptly, "let's get the herd together and get out. The feud is none of my business, and I don't intend to make it mine. Every dime I've got in the world is tied up in that venture."

Tom Kittery looked at him, his eyes suddenly hard. "That's right. It isn't none of your affair, and I'm not expecting you to take a hand in it. Nonetheless, you may have to before we get those cattle out of the state."

Johnny Lubec got up angrily. "I thought you said he was a friend of yours? He sure don't sound like it to me!"

Kittery said nothing, but stared into the fire. Tap Duvarney looked at Lubec. "I consider myself Tom's friend, but that does not involve me in a shooting war that began God only knows how—and years ago, from all I've heard. If I were a member of his family, I might feel otherwise, but I am not. Furthermore, Tom and I made an agreement, and I expect him to live up to it."

"Don't count yourself any friend of mine!" Lubec responded, his tone harsh. "Far as I'm concerned, them as ain't for us is against us."

Tap turned to Kittery, "Tom, if you don't like the sound of this, just give me back my money and we'll forget it."

Kittery looked up. "You know damn well I can't give that money back. I spent it. I bought cattle."

"Then we've got a deal." Tap reached across the fire for the coffeepot. "I'll be ready to go after those cattle in the morning."

"You got to wait." Lubec spoke with cool triumph. "We're goin' after them as killed Foster."

Tap Duvarney sipped his coffee, and when Kittery did not speak he said quietly, "I'll be ready at daybreak, Tom. If necessary, I'll get the cattle out and make this drive on my own; but if I do. I'll sell the cattle and keep every dollar of the money."

"Like hell you will!" Kittery was suddenly angry. "Half those cattle are mine!"

Tap grinned at him. "Don't be a damn fool, Tom. Our deal was my money and your savvy. If you aren't in there working and telling us how, what part can you have? I'm here. My money is in the pot. I made an agreement, and so did you. I understood that in Texas men lived up to their agreements."

"Are you sayin' I don't?"

"I'm saying nothing of the kind. I am only saying that the Munson feud is your personal affair, but I can't let it interfere with my business."

"You're right," Tom said glumly. "Damn it, I am sorry. I got no right to expect you to horn in on my fight."

Johnny Lubec leaped to his feet. "Tom? You backin' down for this—this—"

Tap Duvarney looked up. "Johnny, if you finish that sentence it better be polite or you'd better be reaching for a gun when you say it."

Lubec backed off. "On your feet, damn you! I'll—"

"*Johnny!*" Kittery's voice rang with authority. "Stop it! Tap would kill you before you got a gun out. I've seen him work."

Lubec hesitated, still angry but suddenly wary. Tom Kittery was as near to a God as he could recognize, and if Tom said this stranger was good, he must be good. Abruptly, he turned his back and walked away into the brush.

Tap finished his coffee and got to his feet. "I'm tired. I'm going to turn in."

"Sorry, Tap. Losin' Foster like that—. We're on edge, all of us."

"Forget it."

Tap walked back into the brush and unrolled his bed. He folded his coat neatly, then pulled off his boots and placed them for a pillow. He put his Winchester beside him, and also his gun belt. His spare gun he placed under the blanket and near his hand.

The Cajun came in from watch, drank coffee and ate without talking, and disappeared again. Tom Kittery sat alone by the fire. After a while Lubec returned and crawled into his blankets.

The fire sank low, and Tap slept.

What made him awaken he did not know, but a dark figure loomed above him. The fire was only a few red coals, the columns of the trees against the stars were dark and mysterious. A faint light gleamed on the gun held in the man's hand. The gun was not aimed, it was simply hanging at arm's length against the man's leg. The man was Tom.

Tap's own hand held his gun, pointed up at Kittery through the blanket. "Go to sleep, Tom. You'll feel different in the morning. Besides, this Colt I'm holding on you would rest mighty heavy on your stomach."

Tom Kittery chuckled. "Damn it, Tap, I never knew anybody like you! Nowhere! All right, to hell with the feud! We work cattle."

Tap Duvarney's eyes opened on daylight. For a moment he lay still. The fire had been built up, and he could smell coffee. Lifting his head, he saw the Cajun was slicing bacon into a frying pan. Tap slid out of the blankets and into his boots. Standing up, he slung his gun belt around his lean hips and settled the holster into place against his leg.

He felt good. The air was fresh and cool off the Gulf, not many miles away to the east, and he was a man who had lived most of his life in the open.

The War Between the States had been a blood bath, a desperate, bitterly contested war in which he had been constantly in action, often on secret missions behind the enemy lines. He had been born in Virginia, and his southern accent was a distinct advantage on such jobs. But it was the frontier that honed him down, made keen the edges of his senses, his will to survive. For he had faced the American Indian—a wily, dangerous adversary, a fighting man of the first rank, and one familiar with every aspect of wilderness warfare and survival.

The Cajun glanced up as Duvarney approached the fire. Tap gathered a few sticks for additional fuel and placed them close at hand. It was evidence that he was expecting nobody to serve him. He was here to pull his own weight, no matter what the circumstances.

The future looked bleak enough to him. Every cent he'd owned was tied up in the cattle; a feud and the violent hatreds it generated hung over them. When such a fire burned no man within range was free from it, and the very fact that he was riding with the Kitterys would make him a target. The Kittery faction, too, was filled with hatred. The cattle drive, Tap was quite sure, had been put aside because of the feud; and had he not come along might never have been carried out. They could think of nothing now but striking back, striking hard.

When the coffee was ready, he filled his cup and squatted on his haunches by the fire. Tom Kittery was tugging on his boots. Lubec was nowhere to be seen.

"We got our work cut out for us," Kittery said. "If we round up cattle now we'll be likely to lose 'em.

The Munsons will stampede them some night, scatter 'em from hell to breakfast."

"Then we'll find a place where they can be guarded, and hold them there until we've completed the gather."

"You got any idea what you're gettin' into?" Kittery asked. "Most of those cattle are back in the brush. It won't be easy to get them."

"And you're holding some on Matagorda Island? All right, we'll just round the others up and push them out to the island. Or hold them on Black Jack Peninsula."

Tom Kittery looked over his cup at him. "You said you'd never been in this country before."

"I can read a map," Duvarney answered dryly.

By the time the sun was over the horizon they had pulled out, Duvarney riding the buckboard with Tom Kittery, whose horse was tied behind. The others rode on ahead, or scouted off to one side or the other.

"They're hunting us," Tom said matter-of-factly, "and one day they'll find us. All we've been hoping to do was thin them down a mite before the showdown."

"How many can you muster?"

"Mighty few. Eight or ten at most. We're outnumbered, four or five to one."

"Tough."

They rode on, and from time to time they saw cattle grazing, and several times saw the tracks of horses.

"Comanches raided clear to the Gulf coast some years back," Tom commented, noticing some tracks. "We don't see them any more. At least, I haven't. Back around 1840 they burned Linnville and attacked Victoria. My folks were at Linnville, and nobody expected any Indians. When they came, everybody who could climbed on a barge and pushed out on the water. Saved their lives, but lost everything they had but the land."

"Was Indianola a port then?"

"No . . . not until sometime around 1844, I think. It was started by a German prince, and he called it Carlshafen, after himself, I guess. His name was Prince

Carl Zu Solms-Braunfels. He brought a colony of immigrants into Texas.

"Back in those days they came from everywhere—Germans, French, Swiss . . . we still have a lot of them. Castroville, D-Hanis, Fredericksburg, all those places were settled by foreigners. Over by Fredericksburg half the talk a body hears is in German.

"Indianola picked up for a while, then about 1846 the cholera hit the town—nearly wiped it out. I've heard tell of it. I was too young to remember it."

"Where's Shanghai Pierce's outfit?"

"You've heard of him? I guess ever'body has. He's north of here, up on Tres Palacios Creek. He's got the biggest outfit around here, unless it's Cap'n King." Tom Kittery glanced at Tap. "You two should get along, you going to sea, and all. He was a steamboat captain before he settled in this country. A mighty good man, too. I met him a couple of times."

After this neither man spoke for several miles, and there was no sound but the clop-clop of the horses' hoofs and the jangle of the harness. Johnny Lubec had pulled off and ridden away into the brush. When he returned an hour or so later, he was leading a saddled horse, a tough-looking buckskin with a black mane and tail.

"We'll leave the rig," Tom said to Duvarney. "You'll ride the buckskin."

Tap Duvarney looked doubtfully at the horse, which rolled an inquisitive eye at him as if it had already been informed who its rider was to be, but Tap pulled up and swung down.

"What about the team?"

"We'll take off the harness and turn 'em loose. The buckboard can stay right here in the brush until we have reason to pick it up."

Taking the reins, he drove the buckboard into the brush. Tap took his gear from the wagon, then gestured at the supplies. "I'll need those," he said.

Kittery noticed the ammunition boxes for the first

time. "You figure on usin' all that? What you goin' to do? Fight all the Indians in the Nation?"

Tap shrugged. "They told me you were in a feud. It isn't my fight, but if somebody starts shooting at me I want to be able to shoot back as long as I'm in the mood."

Lubec merely looked at him, while the Cajun took the boxes from the wagon-bed and placed them on the ground. He went to the seat, and from under it he took the sack of oats and dumped what remained on the ground. Then he filled the canvas sack with the contents of the boxes.

With all the packages and sacks loaded behind their saddles and the mustangs turned loose to go home, they took off through the scattered brush and trees. Several times they passed through extensive stretches of prickly pear, and twice they followed stream courses, keeping under the cottonwoods and pecans for concealment.

It was sundown when they rode into a small clearing. For several miles they had been moving through thick brush and timber, and the clearing came as a surprise. There was a small fire going, and three men were standing nearby, all with rifles.

"Howdy, Tom!" A stocky, barrel-chested man with a black beard walked toward them. "Johnny? Howdy, Cajun."

He smiled as he saw Duvarney. "How are you, Major? I never had the luck to run into you during the war, but we came nigh it a time or two. I am Joe Breck."

"You're Captain Joseph Breck? I remember your outfit, sir. I am just as glad we missed our meetings. You had some good men."

Breck smiled. "I've still got a couple of them, and one of yours."

"Mine? Who?"

"Me, Major." A tall, ungainly man with a large Adam's apple stepped from behind a horse he was grooming. "Corporal Welt Spicer."

Duvarney grinned. "How are you, Spicer? I'm not likely to forget you." He looked around at Kittery. "Did he tell you? He was in my outfit. We covered a lot of country together."

Kittery threw a sharp look at Spicer, but made no comment.

The hide-out was a good, if temporary, one. It was on a small knoll in a dense growth of brush; tunnels through the brush showed their dark openings here and there. Obviously the thicket was a network of underbrush passageways and trails. A small spring was nearby, and although the water was brackish, it was potable.

"What's on the program, Tom?" Breck asked.

"We hunt cattle," Kittery replied shortly. "We start at daybreak. We'll make up a herd and strike out for Kansas."

They looked at him, but nobody offered a comment. A few minutes later, Duvarney caught Breck studying Kittery with care. Obviously, Tap thought grimly, he had altered their plans, and they didn't like it.

Tired from the long riding, he rolled up in his blankets. The last he remembered was seeing the others huddled around the fire, drinking coffee and talking in low tones.

Well, he reflected, let them talk. Tomorrow they work cattle.

4

For three days they kept at it, daylight to dark, working the cattle out of the brush, branding them and bunching them at a clearing in the woods that consisted of several hundred acres of good grass, with a trickle of water running across one corner. A few of the cattle still wore the Kittery brand, but most were mavericks.

The work was hard, punishing, and hot, yet they made time. Tap Duvarney had never worked cattle before except on the few occasions when he had hazed a small herd into an Indian camp that was being fed by the government, or when it was cattle to be beefed for the army itself. However, he had watched a lot of cowhands work on the range, and had listened to them yarning over campfires. As he could match none of these men with a rope, he devoted his time to finding the cattle and driving them from the brush or the grassy hollows. By the end of the fourth day they were holding four hundred head of mixed stuff, and their horses were played out.

Most of the cattle had been found within a few miles,

but they were wild, some of them being old mossy-horns that had lived back in the brush for years. These made most of the trouble. At first it was not much more than a matter of riding around the cattle and slowly bunching them; but the older stock would have none of that. Time and again some of the mossy-horns would break for the brush, and it was hard work, and hot work, rousting them out again.

There was no chuck wagon. Every rider carried a small bait of grub in a sack behind his saddle, and ate his noonday meal out on the range . . . if he had time.

On the evening of the fourth day. Kittery said, "We've got to ride for horses. We'll need about forty head, and the nighest place is over to Coppinger's."

"Give you a chance to see Mady," Johnny Lubec said, grinning. "Want I should go along to kind of cool you off after you leave there?"

"I wouldn't trust you. Ever' time we get near the C-Bar, you head for those Mex jackals down in the wash. I think you've got eyes for that little Cortinas girl."

Lubec made no comment, and Kittery said, "All right. We'll ride out at daybreak. Johnny, you can come, and I'll take Pete and Roy." Then he glanced over at Duvarney. "You want to come, Tap?"

"I'll stay here."

After they had gone, Duvarney worked over his guns and equipment, then saddled up to ride out. "I'm going to scout around," he said to the others. "I may drive a few cattle if I see them, but I'm going for a reconaissance."

Welt Spicer got to his feet. "Mind if I trail along?"

"All right with me."

The Cajun watched them with eyes that told nothing, but Joe Breck looked at Duvarney and said, "You be careful. There's Munsons around, and if they see you they'll shoot first an' ask questions afterward."

When they'd been a few minutes on the trail, Welt

Spicer commented, "We're nigh Copano Creek. Empties into the bay yonder."

"Mission Bay?"

"Copano. Mission's smaller, and opens into Copano Bay. . . . You ever been in this country?"

"No, this is my first time east of the Brazos in Texas. But I've seen the maps."

The trail was narrow. Only one rider could follow it at a time, the other trailing behind. Branches brushed them on either side. It was hot and still. The only sound except the muffled fall of their horses' hoofs was the hum of insects or the occasional cry of a bird. Sweat trickled down Duvarney's face and down his body under his shirt. Sometimes they saw the tracks of cattle. Cow trails branched off from time to time, but the riders held to the main trail.

They came on Copano Creek unexpectedly. It was a fair-sized stream, with many twists and turns. Both men dismounted and drank upstream from their horses. The water was clear, and not unpleasant.

"Low tide," Spicer said. "At high tide you can't drink it." He squatted on his heels and took a small Spanish cigar from his pocket. "You got your work cut out for you, Major."

"Call me Tap."

"That Tom, now. He's a mighty good man, but he's mad. He's Munson-killing mad, and so are the others. All of 'em want to fight, not run cattle."

"How about you?"

"I'll string along with you. I figure we're a sight better off drivin' cows to Kansas." Spicer pushed his hat back so he could see Tap's face without tilting his head. "You're goin' to need men—men you can depend on."

It had been that way in the army. There had always been men he could depend on, the right sort of men in the right places when they were needed, and they made easier whatever needed to be done. His had been the responsibility of command, of decision. There had always been the sergeants, many of them veterans of the

War Between the States as well as of Indian fighting. They were tough, dependable men. Now he was alone.

Somehow he had to hold the reluctant men to putting the herd together, somehow he had to get them started on the trail to Kansas. He had to ride rough-shod over their resentment of him, over their hatreds, their reluctance to leave a fight unfinished. It had been easy enough when he had tough non-coms to whom he could relay his orders, and enlisted men whose duty it was to obey. This was different.

He was going to have to get the herd together faster than they had planned, get it ready to move before they expected it. If he started the herd they must come along, like it or not.

"Spicer, you're right. I will need some men. You've been around here a while . . . where can I find them?"

"Fort Brown . . . Brownsville. I happen to know they're breakin' up a cavalry outfit down there, and there'll be some good men on the loose. As far as that goes, there are always a few hands around Brownsville or Matamoras, anyway."

"All right, Spicer. You ride down there. Pick maybe ten good men, thirty a month and found. Tell 'em they may have to fight. But they are hiring out to me—and to me only. You know the kind of men I want. Men like we had in the old outfit."

"It'll take me a week at least. Ten days, more likely."

"Take two weeks if need be, but get the men and get them back up here."

After Welt Spicer had gone, Duvarney rode on along the trail, emerging finally on the lower Copano, and following it along to the bay. He saw cattle from time to time; most of them were unbranded, a few were wearing the Kittery brand, and there was a scattering of other brands unfamiliar to him.

The creek ended in a small inlet, and he cut across to the bay itself. Copano Bay was almost landlocked. From his saddlebag Duvarney took the chart Wilkes had given him and studied the bay, its opening into

Aransas Bay, and the island beyond. All this country was low, probably less than twenty feet above sea level, and much of it was certainly less than half of that.

He made a camp on the shore of the bay, made coffee, and chewed on some jerked beef. He went to sleep listening to the sound of the salt water rippling on the sand, and smelling it. At daybreak he was up, drank coffee, and rode off toward the northeast along the coast.

Several times he saw cattle, and as on the previous day he started them drifting ahead of him, pointing them toward the roundup area. They might not go far, but he might be able to drift some into the country to be covered for the drive. He swam his horse across the inlet at the mouth of the creek and made a swing south to check for cattle tracks on the peninsula that separated Copano from St. Charles Bay. He found a good many, and worked his way back to camp.

Joe Breck was on his feet, rifle in hand, when Tap rode in. "I wondered what happened to you. Where's Spicer?"

"Sent him down to Brownsville."

"You sent him *where?*" Without waiting for an answer, Breck went on, "Tom won't like that."

"He'll like it." Duvarney spoke shortly. "There are a lot of cattle on the peninsula east of us. We'll drift some of this lot in there."

"Wait and see what Tom says," Breck objected. "He's got his own ideas."

"And I have mine. We'll start drifting them in the morning."

Breck stared at him, his eyes level, but Tap ignored the stare and went about getting his bed ready for the night.

"I'll wait and see what Kittery says," Breck said. "He hired me."

"You wait, and then tell him to pay you what you have coming. You won't be working with us any more."

"For a new hand," Breck said, "you swing a wide loop."

"Breck," Duvarney replied, "you're a good man, too good a man to get your back up over nothing. You want to fight the Munsons; but if you do, do it on your own time. They're no damned business of mine, and I'm going to drive cattle. I've got money tied up in this drive, and I can't work up any interest in somebody else's fight."

"It may get to be your fight, too."

"Not if it interferes with this cattle drive. Get one thing through your head. These cattle go to Kansas. If anybody gets in the way, and that means you or the Munsons, I'll drive right over them."

Breck gave him a hard look, but Duvarney paid no attention to it. He rolled up in his bed, and slept.

At daybreak the Cajun had a fire going and coffee on. Duvarney joined him. "Don't you ever sleep?" he asked.

The Cajun grinned; it was the first time Tap had seen any expression on his face. "Time to time," he said. He reached for the pot and filled Tap's cup. "Where do you think we should start?"

Duvarney drew a rough line in the sand. "Ride southeast, start sweeping the cattle north, then turn them into the peninsula."

Joe Breck came up to the fire wearing his chaps and spurs. Thirty minutes later they all rode south to begin working the brush.

It was a wide stretch of country. They rode back and forth, making enough noise to start the cattle moving out of the brush to get away from them, then pushing them toward the cattle trails that led to the peninsula. Some of them would move along those familiar trails easily enough, but a few would be balky. It was little enough the three men could do; but working in that way, there was the chance they could move quite a few head.

It was hot and sticky in the brush. Not a breath of

air stirred. From time to time Duvarney found himself pulling up to give his horse a breather, and each time he did so he turned in the saddle to study the sky. It was clear and blue, with only a few scattered clouds.

They came together on the banks of a small creek flowing into St. Charles Bay, where they made coffee, ate, and napped a little. Through the afternoon they worked steadily, and drifted back into camp at sundown, dead tired.

"We covered some country," Breck commented, "and we moved a lot of beef—more'n I expected."

Tap nodded. He was no longer thinking of cattle. His thoughts had turned back to Virginia, and to the quiet night when he had said good-bye to Jessica Trescott.

Old Judge Trescott, who had known his father—had in fact been his father's attorney—had offered him a job. There were half a dozen others, too, who came up with offers, partly because of his father, and partly because he was to marry Judge Trescott's daughter. He would have none of it. He would take what cash he had, make it his own way.

Was it a desire for independence that brought him west? Or a love of the country itself? Everything he had grown up with was back there in the coast country of Virginia and the Carolinas. His father and his grandfather had operated ships there since before Revolutionary times. There had been Duvarneys trading to the Indies when George III denied them the right. In those days they had smuggled their goods. Duvarneys had been privateers during the Revolution and the War of 1812.

His was an old family on that coast. His service in the War Between the States had been distinguished; on the Indian frontier it had been exceptional in many respects. His position in Virginia was a respected one, and many doors were open to him. Yet he had left. He pulled his stakes and headed west again, to the country he had come to know.

Now here he was, struggling to get a herd together, and so deeply involved that he could not get out of it.

Jessica had rested her hands on his arms that night. "Tappan, if you don't come back soon I'll come after you. No Trescott ever lost a man to a sandy country, and I'm not going to be the first.

"It's no country for a woman," he had objected. "You wait. After I've made the drive and have some cash money, we'll talk."

"You mind what I say, Tappan Duvarney. If you don't come back, I'll come after you!"

He had laughed, kissed her lightly, and left. Perhaps he had been a fool. A man would never find a girl like that in this country. Not even Mady Coppinger.

Tom Kittery would be seeing Mady about now. He was a lucky man, Tap was thinking, a very lucky man.

"Somebody coming," the Cajun said, and vanished into the brush with no more sound than a trail of smoke from the campfire.

Tap listened, and after a moment he heard the faint sounds. One horse, with a rider—a horse that came on steadily at a fair pace and was surely ridden.

He got up and moved back from the flames, and the others did the same.

The rider came on, then drew up while still out in the darkness. "Halloo, the fire! I'm riding friendly, and I'm coming in with my hands empty."

Nobody spoke, and the stranger's horse started to walk. After a moment they could see the rider. He was a stocky, thick-shouldered man with a wide face. Both hands were in the air.

He rode into the firelight and stopped, his hands still held shoulder-high. "I'm hunting Major Duvarney," he said. "Is he here?"

Tap stepped out. "I am Tappan Duvarney."

"And I am Darkly Foster, brother to Lightly Foster, the man you buried at Indianola."

"I know him," Breck said to Duvarney. "He's all right."

" 'Light, and move up to the fire," Tap said. "There's coffee on."

He watched the man lower his hands, and then step down from the horse. It was a fine animal, and Darkly Foster himself moved with a quick ease that told of strong muscles beneath the homespun clothes. "I am sorry about your brother," Tap said.

Darkly turned to him. "No need to be sorry. Lightly lived a full life, and a good one. Feel sorry for those who did him in."

He took a tin cup from his saddle pack and moved to the fire. When he had filled his cup and squatted on his heels he said, "I have come to meet the man who buried my brother. It was a fine thing you did."

Tap filled his own cup. "I never knew him," he said, "but he had the look of a good man."

"He was that. A solid man, a trusted man, and a man of courage. Not many would have dared to do what you did, burying him, with Shabbit and the Munsons looking on. Especially after what happened on the wharf."

"What happened?" Joe Breck asked.

Foster gestured toward Duvarney. "He treated Wheeler and Eggen Munson to a whipping. They started it—picked him for a tenderfoot, and he whipped the two of them so fast he never even mussed his hair. The town's talkin' about it."

"You never mentioned that," Breck commented.

"No need. They were feeling their oats and decided to try me on. Neither one of them could fight."

Joe Breck was silent, and in the silence the fire crackled, and off in the brush one of the horses stamped and blew. A nighthawk wheeled and turned in the sky above.

"Whatever you're planning," Darkly Foster said, "I'll offer a hand. I can use a gun as good as average, and I can handle horses or cattle."

"We're driving to Kansas . . . nothing more."

"You got yourself a hand," Foster said. "I like the way you travel."

It was long after midnight when Duvarney awakened suddenly. The fire had died to coals, with one thin tendril of flame winding itself around a dry branch. The only other man awake was Darkly Foster, who sat across the clearing, back from the fire.

Tap listened for a moment, then sat up and reached for his boots. Riders were coming.

Foster had disappeared from his seat, but could be vaguely seen, well back in the darkness. Duvarney stamped into his boots and skirted the clearing toward Foster.

"It could be Tom Kittery," he said. "He's due back."

They waited. Several horses were coming, moving slowly. When they rounded into the clearing, Tap Duvarney swore bitterly.

Roy Kittery was swaying in his saddle, his face drawn and pale. Pete Remley lay across his saddle, tied on to keep him from slipping off. Tom Kittery had a bloody shirt; only Johnny Lubec seemed to have come off without a wound.

"They were laying for us," Tom Kittery said as he slid from the saddle. "They'd been watching the Coppinger place, and when we left they let us have it. They killed Pete."

Duvarney helped Roy from the saddle. "Get over by the fire, Tom," he said, over his shoulder. "Let's have a look at those wounds."

He turned to suggest the Cajun keep a lookout, but he was gone.

"Did you get any of them?" Breck asked.

"I doubt it. We never even saw them. They were down in the brush off the road, waiting until they had us full in the moonlight. We're lucky to have any of us alive."

Neither Tom nor Roy was hit hard, but Roy had lost a lot of blood. Tap bathed and bandaged the wounds, treating them as well as he could under the circumstances. He'd had a good deal of rough experience in the handling of gunshot or knife wounds, picked up while in the Indian-fighting army.

He was beginning to have his doubts. Nothing was said about the horses they had supposedly gone to get. It began to look as though the group had actually ridden off hunting a fight, or at least hoping to run into some of the Munson party.

Tom Kittery got up and walked to the fire. "It was Huddy," he said bitterly. "Nobody else could have figured it out. Of course, I figured they'd be watching Mady's place, so we didn't go there. We went to a spring up back of the place—at least I did. I left the others a quarter of a mile down the road by a deserted corral. From the spring a man can see Mady's windows on the second floor, and she can see a fire at the spring . . . and there's just no place else a fire like that can be seen. I lit the fire, and Mady came up the slope through the trees about half an hour later and told me it was safe to come on down to the ranch.

"The Coppingers have taken no part in the feud. Fact is, they won't allow me to marry Mady until it is settled, somehow. The Munsons want no truck with them, because the old man has about thirty tough cowhands, and the Munsons don't want to tangle with them.

"I spent the evening there, mostly talking to Mady, then I went back up the hill to the spring, and then back to the corral. The boys had seen nothing and heard nothing. We mounted up and started down the hill toward the Victoria trail. They were waiting for us."

Duvarney stared at him in astonishment. "You blame it on Huddy? How could he know you were there?" He was thinking that Tom Kittery must be naive not to realize that somebody had sold him out; that he had been set up for a killing.

"He's uncanny," Kittery said. "Yes, there's something uncanny about that man," he insisted. "He ain't natural."

Nobody else was saying anything, but from their expressions Duvarney decided they must agree.

"Of course," he said, "I don't know the people on the Coppinger place, but can you trust them?"

Tom Kittery looked at Duvarney in surprise. "Them? Of course. . . . Hell, I'm goin' to marry Mady. That's been understood. It's been an agreed-on thing since before the war."

Duvarney said nothing more. He was an outsider here, knowing nothing of what had gone before, but to him it seemed likely that someone on the Coppinger ranch was accountable for this. He had no faith in the uncanny cunning of Jackson Huddy.

Duvarney was feeling that the sooner he could start the herd out of this country the better. There was too much going on here that was no concern of his, too much that might wreck all his plans. And although he kept trying to force the thought from his mind, he was thinking more and more of Jessica.

Tom looked up at him. "Sorry, Tap. This will hold things up a mite. I mean our getting shot up like this. If you'll just stand by—"

"Stand by, hell! We're going right on with it," Tap said. "When you boys can ride you can join us. I'm still working cattle."

Tom looked sour. "Well, Breck can help, and Spicer." He looked around, suddenly realizing that Spicer was not there. "Where is Spicer?" he asked.

Joe Breck answered. "Duvarney sent him to Brownsville."

"He *what?*" Kittery was angry. "Damn it, Tap, what d'you mean, sending one of my men off?" He paused. "What did you send him for?"

"Men. I'm hiring more men."

Kittery was silent, his face set in hard lines. "You figure to pay them yourself? I hope you've got the money."

"You have, Tom. You've got the money I loaned

you, or whatever of it was saved to finance the drive. You certainly didn't spend it all for cattle."

Joe Breck was staring at the ground, jabbing at it angrily with a stick. Johnny Lubec, hands on his hips, looked equally angry. Duvarney glanced around at the others. He was alone here, that was obvious.

"I figured that money was mine. You bought yourself a partnership," Tom Kittery said.

"I bought half of a cattle drive, not a gun battle. And we'll need some of that money to lay in supplies and pay our way north."

"There's money," Tom protested. "I never used it all. I figured—"

"Whatever you planned, Tom, that money is partnership money, not a war chest."

"All right, all right! Forget it! You want to drive cattle, we drive cattle." Tom looked at Tap. "Damn it, man, I don't want to fight you. If ever a man had a friend, you've been a friend to me. You saved my bacon a couple of times back yonder, and I ain't likely to forget it."

Each morning at daybreak, Tap Duvarney was in the saddle. He drifted cattle toward the peninsula, and several times at low tide he swam his horse across to the island to check the cattle there. Breck or the Cajun worked with him, and when Roy Kittery had regained some strength he worked as well. Lubec was usually off scouting for enemies, and working out a trail by which they might move the cattle without being seen.

It was ten days to the day when Welt Spicer rode into camp. With him were eight rough-looking ex-soldiers, three of them still wearing partial uniform. All of them were armed; all looked fit and ready for whatever came.

Gallagher, Shannon, and Lahey were New York-born Irishmen, Lawton Bean was a long-geared Kentuckian, Jule Simms was from Oregon, and wanted to go back. Doc Belden was a lean, sardonic Texan; and

Judson Walker and Lon Porter were Kansans. All had served in the cavalry against Indians and Mexican bandits, and were veterans of the rough and ready life of the frontier.

Tom Kittery stood beside Tap Duvarney as the men rode in and unsaddled. "With an outfit like that," he said, "we could run those Munsons clear out of the country."

"Forget it. I hired them to run cattle."

"You've made that plain enough," Tom said dryly. "Come on, let's have a cup of coffee and hear what Johnny has to say."

Lubec squatted on his heels and, taking a twig from the fire's edge, traced the route as he talked. "The way I see it, our best chance is to head northwest of Goliad, cross the San Antonio east of there, and strike due north. We're going to have to camp away from streams and hold to sheltered country, but there's a couple of places where we can bed down without being seen unless somebody rides across country."

Lubec paused, and glanced from one to the other. "Unless"—he hesitated—"unless you decide to drive to Indianola and ship from there."

"Indianola?" Tom Kittery shook his head. "It wouldn't work. We'd never make it."

"Look," Lubec suggested. "Before we get that herd together the Munsons will know about it. In fact, they already know we're planning a drive. So they'll be expecting us to try for Kansas. They'd never dream we'd have the nerve to try for Indianola."

"It's a thought," Breck said. "And it just might work."

"Supposing," Lubec went on, "we started our drive like I said, across country to the San Antonio. Then we drive northeast from there, as if we planned to pass Victoria on the south. There's a chance we could pull every Munson out of Indianola and have the cattle in the loading pens there before they knew what had happened."

No one spoke. Tap Duvarney stared into the fire, thinking about the suggestion. It might mean trouble, big trouble; on the other hand, it might mean a quick and adequate return on his money. The profit would not be as great, but neither would the risks be as great as those of the long drive to Kansas and the trail towns.

Indianola was only a few miles away. If the cattle could be driven there, sold there . . .

Then Tom said, "I like it. I think we can do it." He turned to Duvarney. "What about it, partner?"

"Let's wait. We can decide when the cattle start, but once we start nobody leaves the herd, not for any reason at all."

"What's the matter?" Lubec demanded. "Don't you trust us?"

"Do you trust me?" he countered. "If nobody leaves the herd, nobody can talk. It is simple as that."

5

Matagorda was all of seventy miles long, and anywhere from one mile to five miles wide, depending on the state of the tide and the wind. On the Gulf side there were dunes, and a fairly even beach. The west, or landward side, was cut by many little coves or inlets, most of them shallow. There was also a good bit of swampland, with occasional patches of higher, wooded ground. Down the middle of the island was some good grassland, enough to feed a lot of cattle.

It was also a land of catclaw, mesquite, and prickly pear, with the usual allowance of rattlesnakes, jack rabbits, and deer.

Tap Duvarney rode out to the island with Welt Spicer, Jud Walker, and Doc Belden. There were a lot of cattle, most of them wearing the Rafter K, the Kittery brand. Among the others, they found a dozen old cows with calves, carrying no brand at all.

"Doc," Tap suggested, "you're carrying a running iron. You start a fire and heat it up."

Tom Kittery took the makings from his pocket and began to build a smoke. "If you aren't in this fight," he commented, "you'd better ride careful. There's those who wouldn't believe it."

"Tom," Duvarney said quietly, "I know you'd like to have me take up this fight of yours, but I say again that I joined up only for the cattle business. I think this feud is a foolish thing. You and the Munsons are fighting a fight that should have died out years ago. I know they burned you out, I know they killed some of your kin, but you killed some of theirs, too. All I want is to make my drive, and I'd like you to make it with me.

"If we get these cattle to Kansas or sell them in Indianola, whichever proves out, we'll have some cash money, enough to start ranching up north . . . in Wyoming or Montana."

"I'm a Texas man," Kittery protested.

"Hell," Duvarney said, "I've been up there. Half the cattlemen in Wyoming and Montana are from Texas . . . or England. There's good grass up there, and I know the country. We could sell our steers, then drive the young stuff and the breeding stock to northern grass. You could leave this feud behind, own your own outfit, marry Mady Coppinger, and live happily ever after."

"You make it sound good, Tap. You surely do."

"Which sounds better? That, or to roust around the country hunting for Munsons all your life? Until they're all dead, or somebody dry-gulches you?"

"When do you want to pull out?"

"A week from today, with whatever we have. We can try for Indianola if things work out: if they don't, we can strike north for the Red River, fatten our stock on Indian grass, and push into Kansas when the market is right."

Refugio was a sleepy-looking cowtown that belied its appearance. The four riders rode into the dusty street and tied to the hitching rail in front of the courthouse. Boardwalks ran along both sides of the street, and back of the walks were adobe or frame buildings with a few galleries hanging over the walks. The courthouse was open, and Tap strolled across the street and went up the steps. Doc Belden stayed near the horses; Jud Walker and Welt Spicer had gone into the nearest saloon.

"Rocking TD?" The clerk opened the brand book. "I don't recall that one, so you're probably all right on it." He registered the brand, studying the name he had written . . . *Tappan Duvarney*.

"I've heard of you," the clerk commented. "Friend of Tom Kittery's, aren't you?"

"Met him during the war," Duvarney replied.

"He come in with you? If he did, you might tell him Mady Coppinger's in town."

Despite himself, Tap felt excitement. Was it because he hadn't seen any woman in so long? Or—

He shook himself to escape the thought, settled his hat in place, and went out. For a moment he paused in the doorway, his eyes studying the street. One of the ways to avoid trouble was to see it before it got to you.

Doc Belden was still standing near the horses, smoking a small cigar. He was looking down the street toward the saloon, which Tap could not see. Almost without thinking, Tap reached up and unbuttoned his coat. He carried two guns, one in its holster, the other in his waistband.

He walked directly to the horses and stood near Doc. "Everything all right?"

Doc gave him a quizzical glance. "Half a dozen riders just pulled in . . . lathered horses . . . like maybe they'd hurried to get here."

"Mount up," Tap said; "we'll ride down and join the boys."

They tied the horses at the rail in front of the saloon, listening for voices. There were six horses tied nearby; all had been ridden hard, all bore the Circle M brand.

"Sit loose in the saddle, Belden. This may be it, but let me open the ball."

They pushed through the swinging doors into the shadowed coolness of the saloon. Spicer was at the end of the bar, facing the room, and Jud Walker stood close by.

Two of the Circle M riders stood well down the bar from Walker. Two others were seated at a table behind him but about fifteen feet away. The other two were down the room, but facing Walker and Spicer, boxing them neatly.

Tap stepped to one side of the door, his eyes taking in the scene at a glance. Doc Belden had moved easily to the other side of the door.

One of the men at the tables turned his head, squinting his eyes against the outside glare, to see who had come in. It was Shabbit.

"How are you, boys?" Tap said quietly. "Let's all have a drink, shall we?"

The situation had suddenly reversed itself, and it was now the Munson party who were boxed. If they faced the two men at the bar they could not face the two at the door. And shooting against the sunlight was not too easy a thing.

Shabbit hesitated, and the moment passed him by. "To the bar, gentlemen," Tap insisted. "I'm buying the drinks. Bartender, set them up . . . *right there.*"

He was pointing at the center of the bar, and he was pointing with a gun.

Nobody had seen him draw it . . . it was simply there.

One of the Munson men, whom Tap remembered from the graveyard, pushed back his chair and got up. "Don't mind if I do," he said coolly. "You ridin' with the Kitterys now?"

"I'm in the cattle business with Tom Kittery," Tap replied calmly. "I'm not mixed up in any feud, and don't intend to be."

As the first man started to the bar a second man got up. Shabbit was the last to move, muttering under his breath. When all had lined up along the bar and their drinks were poured, Duvarney motioned Walker and Spicer back to the door. Then he went to the bar and paid for the drinks.

"Oblige me, gentlemen," he said, "and stay with your drinks. My finger is very touchy on the trigger, and I'll need at least ten minutes to complete my business here. I would regret killing a man for merely putting his head out of the door."

Retreating to their horses, they mounted and walked them slowly down the street. They left town on the road to Victoria, but soon turned off it and went toward the San Antonio River. It was after dark when they made camp in the breaks along the San Antonio, and before daylight they were moving again. By late morning they were riding into Victoria.

Spicer and Walker stayed with the horses, while Duvarney and Doc Belden walked down the street. Mady Coppinger was on the boardwalk on the other side. Tap crossed over, removed his hat, and bowed.

"Miss Coppinger?" he said. "It is good to see you again."

His eyes went up and down the street, scanning the buildings, even the second-story windows.

"I don't understand you, Major Duvarney. Why would a man like you want to come to Texas? Tom says you have connections in Virginia, that you've lived all over, know all sorts of people."

"I like Texas."

"You *like* it? I find that hard to believe."

"It's a man's country, I will admit, but you would find the cities less attractive after you had been there a while."

"Anything is better than this," she replied. "I wish . . . I wish I could just move away and never see it again. You men may like the dust, the cattle, the sweating horses . . . I don't. I want to be where there's life . . . excitement."

"You would find it just as dull there after a while,"

Tap commented. His eyes swept the street again. "Have you time to eat with me? I see there's a restaurant up the street, and I'd be pleased if you'd be my guest."

"I'd like that very much," she agreed, "after I get some things I need." While she went on down the street to do her shopping, Tap Duvarney walked back to the horses.

"We'll be in town for a bit," he said. "I'm going to have dinner with Miss Coppinger."

"You sure do pick 'em, Major," Walker said, grinning. "That's a mighty handsome figure of a woman."

"She's spoken for," Duvarney replied shortly. "That is the girl Tom Kittery is going to marry."

"You'd never know it, the way she was lookin' at you," Jud commented. "But that's none of my affair." He looked around uneasily. "You want us to stay close? I smell trouble."

"There's a grove of pecans on the edge of town. After you boys do whatever buying there's to do, meet me there . . . in an hour."

Welt Spicer hesitated. "You sure you don't want us to stay by you? I've heard tell this here is a Munson town."

"No . . . just be there when I come. I'll be all right."

The restaurant was a small place, with white curtains at the windows and white tablecloths and napkins. Mady came in a moment after he arrived, moving gracefully. Her eyes lighted up when she saw him. "You may not believe this," she said, "but I've lived near Victoria all my life and this is only the second time I have eaten here."

He glanced at her thoughtfully. She was uncommonly pretty, and especially so today. She was, he thought, one of those girls who love company, who like to be going and doing. There was little chance of that on a cattle range.

"But you're in town often," he protested. "Where do you eat?"

"We bring our lunch. But sometimes we eat at the

home of friends." She looked up, her blue eyes resentful. "You haven't been here long enough to know, Major Duvarney, but cash money is hard to come by in Texas these days. My father has more cattle than most folks around Victoria, but he sees very little cash money. I had to skimp and save to make that trip to New Orleans. Not that pa isn't well off," she added. "It's just the way things are in Texas."

She looked unhappy, and it caused him to wonder about her relationship to Tom Kittery. Tom was the sort of man who would appeal to women. He was tall and well set-up, he carried himself with a manner, and had an easy, devil-may-care way about him. His family had standing in East Texas, and but for the feud might have been living in prosperity ... on a par with her own family.

Obviously, that was not enough for Mady Coppinger. She wanted the life of the city and its real or fancied excitements. Her one brief visit had only served to whet her appetite for more, and had been brief enough to bring no disillusionment. Such a girl was the last person in the world for Tom Kittery, a man committed by birth and inclination to the wilder West.

"Cities aren't the way you seem to think them," he said, "and most of the people living there have no part of what is supposed to be the glamour and the excitement. You probably have a better life and a more interesting life right here."

They talked on, and in spite of himself he was led to talk of New York and Washington, of Richmond and Charleston. The time went by too quickly, and more than an hour had passed before he broke away and joined his men, who were growing restive.

He had learned a little. Mady was in love with Tom, but was torn between her love for him and her desire to be rid of Texas and all it stood for. She loved him in her way, but she wanted him away from Texas, and she doubted his ability to win the feud. The fighting itself disturbed her less than he expected, yet somewhere, somehow, she had been offered some powerful and fairly consistent arguments to indicate that Tom had no chance of winning.

He had a feeling that when she talked of this she was not using her own words, but words she had heard. From her father, perhaps? Or from somebody else? Had Tom any inkling of her doubts? Or that there might be some who lacked faith, someone close to Mady or himself?

He had no doubt that somebody had informed the Munsons that he and his men had ridden to Refugio the day before. Those hard-ridden horses were hard to explain in any other way.

Somebody had informed the Munsons in time for them to get some fighting men to Refugio. That they had failed in their mission was largely due to the fact that they had failed to catch Duvarney and his men together in a single group.

Tap Duvarney had lived too long to trust anyone too much. It was his nature to like people, but also to understand that many men are weak, and some are strong. In the rough life of the frontier strengths and weaknesses crop out in most unexpected places, and there is less chance to conceal defects of character that in a less demanding world might never become known . . . even to their possessor.

Someone close to Tom Kittery, someone whom he trusted, was betraying him. It would pay to ride carefully and to study the trail sign before revealing too much to anyone.

Riding back to the hide-out in the brush, Tap Duvarney considered his moves with care, trying to foresee the moves the enemy would make, and to plan his own accordingly.

They must do the unexpected, always the unexpected.

Tom Kittery got up from the fire and approached as Tap swung down. "We'll drive for Kansas," Tap said, "and we'll start day after tomorrow."

6

Over the sullen coals of a mesquite-root fire, Tap Duvarney told his men: "Roll out at first light, bunch on Matagorda, and sweep south. Start about here." He drew a rough map of the island. "Push down and swim them over to here."

He turned to Kittery. "Tom, how about you taking your boys and sweeping kind of east by north from Copano Creek? Scatter out and gather what you can, but waste no time chasing the tough old ones.

"Darkly Foster can take Shannon, Lahey, and Gallagher over to the tip of Black Jack Peninsula and drive north. We'll work fast and we'll miss a lot of stuff, but we should rendezvous on Horseshoe Lake with a good-sized herd."

Kittery nodded. "Seems likely. How about you?"

"I'll take Doc, Lawton Bean, Spicer, and Jule Simms over to the island. Walker and Porter can work with you."

"You'll never make it. Not in the time you're givin' us. That's a whole lot of country."

"I know it is, and we can't make a clean sweep. Just start driving and keep moving. What we get we'll take, and what's left we can get the next time."

"All right, Major," Kittery said ironically, "you're givin' the orders."

Breck and Dubec stared stubbornly at the ground, ignoring Tap. The Cajun showed no feeling one way or the other. Tap said mildly, "If we all do our part, this should be quite a drive. We'll slip out of here without a fight."

Lubec laughed contemptuously. "You don't know them Munsons, Major." Lubec emphasized the title. "They'll wait until you bunch your stock and they'll move. You'll see."

"I hope you'll be there shooting when they do, Johnny," Tap replied pleasantly. "Now I'm going to hit the hay. I'm tired."

Slowly, they drifted away to their beds, all but Breck, Lubec, and Kittery.

"They don't like it much, Major," Spicer whispered, "you takin' command like this."

The night was still. The crickets' chirping was the only sound. Tap clasped his hands behind his head and stared up at the stars, which winked occasionally through the black mantilla formed by the branches and leaves overhead. He liked the smell of the earth, the trees, the coolness of a soft wind from off the Gulf.

Despite his outward assurance, he was far from confident. There were too many things that could happen, too many things to go wrong, and there was too much that was doubtful about his own relationship with Tom Kittery.

The man was moody and solitary, and when not alone he kept close to those who had been with him from the beginning. The bitterness of the feud was upon him, the memory of good men dead, of his burned-out home, of the graves of his family. Nor could Tap blame him. In Tom's place, he too would have fought. But he was not in Tom's place.

His future lay in that herd of cattle they were to gather, his future and perhaps that of Jessica. He wanted to return to her without empty hands, and if he could not return that way, he made up his mind suddenly, he would not go back at all.

He was too proud to accept a position from her family, or from friends of either his family or hers. His father and grandfather had walked proudly, had made their own way, and so would he make his. He could return to the service, but he knew what it meant —fighting Indians or living out a dull existence on some small post on the frontier.

With the few men they had, they could not hope to make anything like a clean sweep. They could only do their best, then move the herd; with luck they would get out without a fight. He was not at all as hopeful of that as he had sounded at the campfire.

Finally he slept. In the night he stirred restlessly, the sea in his bones responding to something on the wind, some faint whisper from out over the wastes of the ocean. Something was happening out there, something he knew by his instincts. Several times he muttered in his sleep, and when he awakened he was not refreshed.

The Cajun was at the fire. Did the man never sleep at all? He looked up at Duvarney and, taking his cup from his hand, filled it from the coffeepot.

Brooding, the Cajun sipped at his coffee. Presently he glanced around at Duvarney. He nodded to indicate a huge log that lay over against the edge of the clearing. It was an old log measuring at least four feet through, and was perhaps sixty feet in length.

"He big tree . . . grow far off."

Tap Duvarney looked at the log. It certainly was larger than anything he had seen along the Gulf Coast, although there might be something as big in the piney woods to the north.

"How did it get here?"

The Cajun jerked his head toward the Gulf. "Storm. Big storm bring him on the sea."

Tap looked at the log again. They were at least five miles from the Gulf Coast. To come here by sea, that log would have to cross Matagorda Island and then be carried this far inland.

"Have you seen the sea come this far in?"

"One time I see. My papa see, also. One time there was a ship back there." He turned and pointed still further inland. "Very old ship. It was there before my grandpa."

The Cajun relapsed into silence over his coffee. There was no light in the sky, but a glance at his watch showed Duvarney that the hour was four in the morning. When he had finished his coffee he went out and caught up his horse, then bridled and saddled him.

Standing beside the horse, he thought over the plans he had made. There was much about them he did not like, but he could see no alternative that would improve the situation.

The night coolness had gone. The air was still, and it was growing warmer. He led his horse back and tied him to a tree not far from the fire.

He accepted a plate of beef and beans from the Cajun, and ate while the others crawled sleepily from their beds. It was going to be a long, hard day.

There is no creature on the face of the earth more contrary than the common cow. Not so difficult as a mule, not so mean or vicious as a camel, the cow beast can nevertheless exhaust the patience of a Job.

Duvarney and his men started on the island, and contrary to his announced intention, they did not drive south, but north.

It was not until they reached the island that Tap pulled up and hooked a leg around the saddle-horn. He pushed his hat back and got a small cigar from his pocket. "We're going to do a little different from what I said." He paused to strike a match. "We're going to drive the cattle north, cross from the tip of the island over to the mainland, at low tide or close to it, and take our part of the herd right into Indianola."

"Suits me," Spicer commented.

"Me too," Doc said. "We'll get to town that much sooner."

"Somebody," Duvarney went on, "has talked too much, or else somebody has too much confidence in their friends. So if you should meet anybody, don't let them get the idea we're driving north."

"That's marshy country," Jule Simms said doubtfully. "We're liable to bog down the herd."

Tap reached into his saddlebag and brought out a folded chart, now much crumpled. "Look here," he pointed. "This is an old smugglers' trail. It was an Indian trail before that. We'll have to watch the herd, but if we keep them on that trail we can go right through."

They scattered out and began to work back and forth across the island, pointing the cattle north. Here and there other brands were found, and those they cut out and turned back. It was slow, painstaking work. The cattle were loath to be driven, stubbornly resisting, and a few were allowed to go.

The weather was hot and sultry. Not a breath of air circulated among the low-growing brush, or moved in from the sullen sea. Tap mopped his face again and again, fighting the flies, but he kept driving the cattle out. By noon they had a good-sized herd moving up the island ahead of them.

Jule Simms had gone back for fresh horses, and they took a long nooning by a brackish waterhole near Panther Point. Kittery was to have started horses to them, and with luck Simms would meet them halfway.

Lawton Bean held his cup in his gnarled, work-hardened fingers "You figure this'll turn into a scrap?" he asked.

"Not if I can help it," Duvarney said. And then he added, "But I'd say the odds were against us making it all the way without a fight."

"You figure to drive the other herd thisaway?"

Duvarney shook his head. "No . . . and this isn't

to be talked about. We'll drive this bunch in and sell them right in Indianola. If things work the way I figure, they already know we've a drive under way over on the Copano; and unless I'm mistaken, that will pull all the Munson crowd out of Indianola."

The grass was good, and the cattle, fortunately, showed no inclination to go back. When Duvarney had put out the fire and they had saddled up again, they merely nudged the cattle along. On the landward side of the island there were inlets and coves, and small scattered lakes, and the cattle took shelter from the flies in some of the thick brush there. But Duvarney led the way, working the reluctant cattle out of the brush and starting them north.

Welt Spicer met him at the end of one of the narrow necks of land that lay between the ponds and lakes. He mopped his face and swore. "Hotter'n hell," he said. "Cyclone weather, if I ever did see it."

"Jule should be along," Duvarney said. He stood in his stirrups, but it offered him no advantage. He could see nothing but the tops of willows. "My horse is played out," he added.

"So's mine. How far to the end of the island?" Spicer asked.

"Twenty miles."

"We ain't goin' to make it today. Maybe not tomorrow."

"Tomorrow. We should cross over to the mainland before noon. The brush thins out further along, and the island narrows down. I'm going to send you and one of the other boys ahead to keep the cattle to the Gulf side of the island."

Their horses started reluctantly. A big red steer lifted his head and stared at them defiantly. His horns would spread an easy seven feet; he would weigh fifteen hundred pounds if an ounce, and all of it ready for trouble. Both men started for him and he lowered his head a little, then thought better of it and turned away.

Spicer started a cow and a calf from the brush, the

cow wearing the Rafter K brand, as the steer had. "We'll get that brindle calf in the roundup," Spicer said.

They had moved no more than two miles from their nooning when Simms caught up with them, bringing ten head of horses.

Tap Duvarney stripped his saddle from his own weary horse and saddled one of the new ones—a strawberry roan with three white stockings. It was a mustang, but there had been some good blood in it somewhere, for the horse had fine lines. It looked strong and tough.

Jule Simms sat his horse, studying Duvarney. "I heard some talk," he said at last.

"I'll listen."

"They're goin' to kill you—Breck an' them."

Tap rested his hands on the saddle and looked across the horse at Simms. "Do they know you heard this?"

"I was saddling a horse—they didn't even know I was around. They want you out of the picture. With you gone, they figure to fight the Munsons."

"Does Tom know this?"

"Not from the way they talked. Of course, I couldn't say for sure. Breck hates you for bein' a Yankee-lover, and Lubec thinks you rate yourself too high. Mostly they think you're ridin' roughshod over Tom and keepin' them from killin' Munsons."

"Do you know just what they're planning?"

"I didn't hear that part, only it's supposed to come soon. Maybe at Horseshoe Lake, maybe somewhere else."

"Thanks, Jule," Duvarney said. "Thanks."

"The boys and me, we figure you're our boss. We're riding for you. If you want us to, you say the word and we'll ride down there and talk it over some."

"I appreciate that. I surely do." Tap stepped into the saddle. "Let's get on with the drive."

Several times he came within sight of the Gulf. The sea looked sullen and heavy. The water scarcely rustled on the sandy beach. He drew up, smelling the air and looking seaward. There was a sort of swell to the sea, scarcely discernible.

The island had narrowed, and the cattle could be moved faster. He threw himself into the work.

Lawton Bean rode in, hazing a mixed lot of stuff, mostly young, with a couple of old mossy-horns. He had been working among the tide-water ponds and stringers of land that ran out among the maze of inlets and channels along the inland shore of Matagorda. His faded blue shirt was dark with sweat, and the dust on his face was streaked with it.

"I swear that Tom Kittery must've branded everything that wore hair!" he said. "A couple of times back in the brush I'm sure I seen a cougar wearin' his brand."

"There was a cowhand over on the Nueces one time roped and branded a razor-back hog," Simms commented.

"Now, that ain't a-tall likely," Bean objected. "You ever try to dab a rope on a hog? He holds his head down too low. I'd say a man ropin' one of them razor-backs had his work cut out for him."

"There was a hand rode for King Fisher down around Uvalde would dab his rope on anything he could get his loop over. He roped a buzzard one time. It had got so full of meat off a dead crittur it couldn't get off the ground."

"How many head we got up there?" Simms asked. "We must have half the stock in East Texas."

"There's a few hundred head," Duvarney said, cautiously.

"You countin' deer?" Bean asked. "We got four, five head of deer in among them cows."

Welt Spicer drifted in, pushing a few head, among them a huge red steer that stood all of seventeen hands high and carried a magnificent head of horns. He rolled his eyes and bobbed his head at them, but went on by.

"Any you boys want some exercise, you might try

ropin' Big Red there. He don't take to it," Spicer said.

"Knew a cowhand one time over in the brush country," Lawton Bean said, starting to build a smoke. "He was a reliable man. You sent him out to do something, he done it, no matter what. Well, one time the boss told him to clean up all the stock south of the ridge, and when he came in that night he had a hundred and twenty-seven head of cattle, thirty sheep, three mountain goats, seven tom turkeys, a bobcat and two bears . . . and what was more, he'd branded ever' last one of them."

"I don't believe that part about the sheep," Jule Simm said mildly. "Seems unlikely a man would run sheep with cows."

Tap Duvarney looked around, and found a sheltered spot near some dunes, with the Gulf waters within view. There was driftwood about, and some brush. "We'll camp right here," he said, "and make a small fire. We'll take turns on guard tonight."

"You goin' on in tomorrow?" Spicer wanted to know.

"Uh-huh . . . right in. We'll hold the herd a few miles out and I'll go on in and make a deal." He looked around at them as they stripped their gear from the horses. "From here on in, you boys act like you're expecting Comanches. You'll earn your wages before we leave Indianola, unless I'm mistaken."

"How about the cattle? Will that water be shallow enough?"

"For them?" Welt Spicer grinned at the speaker. "Mister, those cattle don't know whether they'd rather graze on the prairie or the ocean bottom. They swim like fish. Shanghai Pierce calls his sea lions. You'll see why."

Jule Simms took over the cooking. Earlier in the day he had shot a deer, and they ate venison and the remains of the *tortillas* they had brought along, and drank coffee. Doc Belden strolled down to the edge of the water and for some time they could see his dark figure against the steel gray of the Gulf. When he came back, he said, "Let me have first watch. I'm not tired."

The fire died down, the men rolled up in their blankets, tired out with the day's work. Tap walked to the brackish pond and washed his face and hands. When he went back to the fire all the men were asleep but Doc, who was up on the side of a dune with his Winchester.

"What's the 'Doc' stand for?" Tap asked him.

"Courtesy title. I had a notion back when I was a youngster that I wanted to take up medicine. I read for it, worked four years with a doctor . . . a damned good one, too."

"What happened?"

Doc Belden glanced at him. "I was a kid. The girl I thought I was in love with married somebody else, so I pulled my freight. Away down deep I think that was what I wanted anyway. I wasn't cut out for a home guard. The army was recruiting, so I joined up. I did a year at Fort Brown, and then they transferred a few of us west. I was at Fort Phil Kearney when Carrington was in command."

After that they sat silent for a time, staring out to sea. The night was cool, the sea calm except for that slight persistent swell.

Tap indicated the Gulf. "I don't like the look of it . . . too quiet."

"I know nothing about the sea."

"That's where I started."

Tap continued to stare seaward. It was a lovely night, with a young moon high in the sky. "There's something going on out where that swell comes from."

He got to his feet. "If there's trouble, I'll be sleeping yonder, and I'm a light sleeper."

He went down the dune, checked the coffeepot, and added a little water and a little coffee for the guards to come. The cattle had wandered off toward the north, and only a few were in sight. There was grass up where they had bedded down, and he doubted if any would start back before daybreak.

He checked his gun, then peeled of his coat and sat down, tugging at his boots. How many times had he slept out as he was sleeping now? And how many times would he do so in the future? Belden was one of those who did not fit . . . he was a square peg, and content to be so. Was he, Tap Duvarney, a square peg? If so, he was not content. He wanted a home . . . and he wanted Jessica.

How long he had been asleep he did not know, but when a hand touched his shoulder gently, he opened his eyes at once, his fingers already closing on the butt of his gun.

It was Lawton Bean, who was to stand the third watch. Tap's mind put that together, and he noticed the position of the stars . . . it was within an hour of daybreak.

"Major," Bean said in a low tone, just loud enough for Duvarney's ears. "There's somebody out there . . . somebody on a horse."

7

Tap Duvarney threw back his blanket and got to his feet. For a moment he listened, hearing nothing. He glanced toward the fire, now a bed of red coals. The scattered sleepers were all hidden from sight in the deeper shadows. He sat down again and tugged on his boots, then thrust his gun down into his belt, and picked up his gun belt and holster.

"South?"

"Yes . . . close by."

They walked away from camp, keeping to the brush shadows. To the south there was an open space of about three acres, all grass well eaten down. Farther to their right, which was the inland side, there were tall reeds along what was called Pringle Lake, which was actually an almost landlocked cove.

The approach from the south was difficult, which was one reason for Duvarney's choice of the position. The night was clear and the stars were out, but the moon was now low in the sky and not of much help. However, the sea and the sand reflected enough light to make anyone hesitant about attempting an approach.

The two men stood there together, waiting. After a moment or two they heard a sound, the same sound Bean had heard before. It was the whisper of brush over coarse denim . . . and then the slightest jingle of a spur. A rider was coming up from the south, walking his horse.

Lawton Bean watched the shadow take shape. "It ain't the same one, Major, I'll take an oath."

"I believe you." He hesitated. He had a pretty good idea who it was now; he even believed he could see the horse. "You go back on watch, Bean," he said. "Keep a good lookout."

Tap waited, standing there alone, watching the rider come nearer. When the horse was still a little distance off he spoke. "Come on in, Tom, with your hands empty."

Tom Kittery rode on up, reining his horse in as he neared Duvarney. "Hey, you mean it!"

"Yes, I mean it, Tom. Some of your boys are after my scalp."

"My boys? You're crazy!"

"They want to fight, Tom. They want to push that feud. They also want me out of the way, because they think I'm blocking them."

Tom Kittery chuckled. "Well, ain't you?" He pushed his hat back, curled a leg around the saddle-horn, and started to build a smoke. "You can't blame them, Tap. They've lost people to the Munsons, same as I have. They figure you're an outsider."

"You tell them to lay off. Tell that to Lubec and Breck, and whoever. I haven't got time to fight, but if they push me, they can get it."

"You surely ain't changed," Kittery said. "You always was a right smart fightin' man, Tap. They got that to learn."

He glanced around. "You're pushing north?"

"Uh-huh . . . I'm going to sell cattle in Indianola

while they're watching you at Horseshoe Lake, or about there."

"Canny . . . you always was a canny one. How many head you got?"

"Eight, nine hundred. Mixed stuff."

Tom drew on his cigarette, and the end glowed in the darkness. "Sorry to say this, boy, but you got to go back. There's no trail across the swamps."

"There's a trail. Just don't you say anything about this when you get back to camp."

At Tom's odd look, Duvarney added, "You've got a spy in camp. Or somebody who comes to camp now and again. They almost had us in Refugio, and they knew we were coming."

"One of my boys?" Kittery shook his head. "I won't take stock in that, Tap. I know my outfit. They've been with me for years."

"They haven't been with me, and I *don't* know them. No matter. . . . Those riders had to run their horses half to death to get to Refugio in time to meet us."

Tom Kittery said nothing, but Tap knew he was irritated. Tom trusted his friends, and he wanted to hear nothing against them.

Tap changed the subject. "How does it happen you ride in here at night? Is something wrong over yonder?"

"Mady's lit out. Her pa came into camp just a-foamin' and a-frettin'. Figured she'd come to me, but she sure enough hadn't, so I came over here."

"Here?"

Tom rested his left hand, holding the cigarette on his knee, which was still around the saddle-horn.

"Heard you was with her in Victoria," he said mildly. "I figured maybe you two had somethin' goin'."

"Don't be a damn fool, Tom, and don't try snapping that cigarette in my eyes when you go for your gun, because it won't work."

Tom gave another chuckle. "Canny . . . that's what I said. She ain't here, then?"

"She wouldn't come here, Tom. We talked a little, that was all. I'm an engaged man, Tom, and I take it seriously. I wouldn't start anything with the girl of a friend, anyway."

"All right. You say that, but what about Mady? She's forever talkin' of city folks and their ways . . . and you especially, ever since you came."

"Well, she's not here, Tom. Forget it, and let's go have some coffee."

They went into camp together and took their cups to the fire. The coffee was black and strong.

Hunching down by the fire, Duvarney studied Tom Kittery carefully. The man looked thinner, harder. He looked like a man with an edge to him, a man ready to strike out suddenly, violently. And Tom Kittery, at any time, was a dangerous man.

"Let's get some sleep." Tap drained his cup and threw the dregs into the fire. "You can use Bean's bed."

"I got one." Tom got up slowly. "If you ain't seen her I just don't know where to look."

Tap sat down and started to tug off his boots. Then suddenly he went cold and clammy. That other sound —the one Lawton Bean said he had heard before . . .

Tom Kittery would never believe Tap had told the truth if Mady Coppinger rode into camp. Or if he awakened to find her there in the morning.

Tap sat there, feeling the damp chill, holding a boot in his hand. Across the camp he could see Tom Kittery unrolling his blanket and tarp.

Behind him, Tap heard something stir in the sand.

Inwardly he cursed, suddenly, bitterly. Leave it to a woman to get a man killed. What had she run away for, anyway? Some fool notion about going to the city, as if that was the answer for everything. In a city, without family or connections or money, there was only one way for a girl to go.

He was tired, dead tired, but he'd be damned if . . . Behind him he heard a faint whisper. Or had he imagined it?

Deliberately, he got up and crossed to the fire, filling his cup at the pot. The coffee was strong enough to stiffen the hair on a man's neck, and hot enough to scald. He tasted it, then put the cup down.

He had no intention of being killed or of killing anyone over Mady Coppinger. If that had been her back there . . . but suppose it was somebody else? Some wounded man, trying to reach him? He shook off the idea, and picked up the coffee cup. He needed sleep. He was desperate for it.

He sat quietly and now sipped the coffee. At last he put the cup down and, after rinsing it, he walked back to his blankets and crawled into them, boots and all. Almost instantly, he was asleep.

When he awoke it was broad daylight and the camp was still. He sat up, blinking and looking around. His horse was saddled and tied nearby, the coals were smoldering, and the coffeepot was still on the fire. Everyone was gone.

He got up, shook out his blanket, and rolled it in his tarp. Under a stone beside the fire there was a note, hurriedly written.

Figgered to let you sleep. Else you ketch up, we will hold this side of Bayucos. K still around.
Spicer

Getting some jerked beef and hardtack from the saddle-bag, he squatted on his heels and chewed the beef, ate the hardtack, and swallowed the coffee which was bitter as lye. But it was hot, and he enjoyed it.

Finally he took the pot off the coals and covered the fire with sand. While the pot cooled off, Duvarney looked about the place where his bed had been. He could not be sure, but it looked suspiciously as if somebody had come up behind him in the soft sand.

He packed the coffeepot, then swung into the saddle and started north. The sand was so chewed up by cattle tracks that there was no possibility of reading sign.

He took his time. The occasional glimpses he had of the sea worried him. The swell had grown larger rather than diminishing, and the water still had that same glassy appearance. The sky was vague, the horizon indistinct.

The western side of the island grew more and more boggy, and the line of cattle slimmed down until at places it was moving almost in single file. Twice he saw places where animals had been dragged from the swamp. Where they had held closer to the Gulf side of the island, they had moved steadily along.

They were nooning and had a fire going when he rode up to them. "By Jimminy," Simms said, "there's our coffeepot!"

"Thanks, boys. I enjoyed the coffee."

"I crossed up yonder," Lawton Bean said. "It ain't bad a-tall. There's a few young uns we may have to pack over on our saddles, but otherwise it's a cinch."

"You boys go ahead. I'm going to scout trail."

He rode on, leaving them around the fire, and pushed through the cattle and crossed to the mainland. At this hour there was only one place where his horse had to swim, and the water was lower than his chart had told him. He was riding up on the shingle when he saw the tracks.

A horse had come this way not long after daybreak, to judge by the tracks—a freshly shod horse with a smaller, neater hoof than Bean's horse.

There were some wind-blown trees back from the crossing place, and he headed for them, wanting to take a sight over the route that lay ahead. After all, his chart was not new, and swampland could change. He had gambled on that trail.

Suddenly he glimpsed a horse and rider among the trees ahead. He turned his mount to weave around some small brush, and when his gun hand was on the side away from the trees he slipped the thong. He planned to use the gun he carried behind his belt, but a man never knew.

His horse scrambled up the sandy slope and into the trees, and he saw that the rider was Mady Coppinger.

"Tap," she said at once, "you've got to help me."

He pulled up six or seven feet away, his eyes scanning the brush behind and all around her. "What can I do," he asked, "that Tom Kittery can't do?"

"You can help me get out of here. I want to go to New Orleans."

"It's no place for a girl without family or friends," he said. "How could you make a living?"

"Oh . . . oh, I'll find a way!" She was impatient. "Tap, I just can't stand it any longer! I can't stand everybody going to bed when the sun's scarcely out of the sky. I want to go somewhere where there are lights and music, and something is happening. I'll just die here!"

"Have you talked to Tom about it? He's figuring on getting married. He wants to live in this country; and besides, it's the only life he knows."

"I don't care about Tom." Her chin went up. "I'm finished, Tap. Do you hear? Finished!" She swung her horse nearer. "Tap, if you'll take me to New Orleans I can go. I'll . . . I'll do anything you want."

"You've got a good man," he said roughly, "and no town is like you seem to think it is. They're all the same unless you have money; and going the way you are talking of, you simply wouldn't have any.

"Anyway, what makes you think you'd see any of the life you're thinking about if some man took you to New Orleans; or anywhere else? He might rent a house and just leave you there to visit when he pleased. He might not take you anywhere."

"I'd leave him!"

"For somebody else like him? Mady, you're too smart a girl to do anything so foolish. You've got something here—a good man who wants you, a recognized position, with family and friends around. You'd be throwing it all over . . . for what? To live in a city where all the doors that mattered would be closed to you. Stop being a damn fool and go home."

She stared at him, her face white with anger. Her lips curled. "I thought you were really something! I thought you were the man I wanted, you with your city ways and your style! You talk like a preacher!" Her tone was thick with contempt. "I've had too much of that at home. I wouldn't go with you now if you begged me!"

He reined his horse around. "I haven't begged you, Mady. I haven't even asked you."

Ten minutes later, he came to the spot marked on the chart for the trail's beginning. It was overgrown with grass, but it showed evidences of recent use, more than likely by Indians going to the shore for the fishing, for there had surely been little other travel this way.

He tied his handkerchief to a bush to mark the opening, then rode out along the trail, scouting the way. At this time of year the swamp did not look bad, and it was possible there might be several routes that would take them through. Nonetheless, he held to the trail, emerging from it several miles further along, near the head of Powderhorn Lake.

He found a place among the willows near the lake and made a concealed camp there, starting a small fire. This spot could be no more than five miles from Indianola, and it would be easy travel from here into the port. Yet he felt worried and restless. So far all had gone well, and his ruse might have taken the Munson men out of the port city, but there was no certainty of that.

Tap Duvarney knew what remained. He must ride into town with at least one man who would know the Munsons when he saw them. That man would be Spicer. He might take one other. He would try to make a quick deal, then when they got their cash the lot of them would move out to join Tom Kittery and the main herd.

The cattle started to come, and he rode out to intercept the leaders and turn them. The grass was good at the head of Powderhorn, so the cattle settled down to grazing. Lawton Bean was the first man to appear. Together they held the cattle while the rest of the herd streamed in from the narrow trail. There had been no trouble. It was all too easy; and to Tap Duvarney, to whom few things had come easy, it only served to worry him still more. Something had to be wrong, or to go wrong. Things simply didn't happen this way.

"I was glad to get off that island," Doc Belden commented as he drew abreast. "You should see the way the sea is breaking out there. Smooth as glass, but great big swells . . . biggest I ever saw."

"Doc," Tap said, "I'm going to leave you in charge of the herd. They'll be uneasy, with the weather changing, so you'll have to hold them close. I'll take Welt Spicer and Lawton Bean."

Doc Belden tamped his pipe thoughtfully. "Spicer should know the Munsons. He's been around long enough, but you be careful."

"I'm going to turn a fast deal if I can. It may not be the best one, but it will be fast and it will give us some more working capital.

"Doc," he added, "Mady Coppinger is around. She's Tom's girl, but she's got some fool notion about running off to New Orleans. Tom's hunting her, and she's ready to jump at any chance to get away from here. Be careful . . . it's a killing matter if she's found with anybody.

"I told him I hadn't seen her, and I hadn't then, but now she's been close to camp and I've talked with her. She's mad enough to bite nails."

"Leave it to a woman to cause trouble," Doc Belden said. "All right, Tap, you go on in when the boys get here. We'll watch things here. Only don't be gone too long. I don't like the looks of the weather out there."

It was a short ride to Indianola.

8

Jackson Huddy did not leave Indianola when the others did.

Deliberately, he remained behind, disliking to trust his safety to such a group, with its accompanying noise, idle talk, and carelessness. He preferred to depend on his own sense, his own instincts.

His were the feelings of a prowling carnivore. He preferred to travel alone, to hunt alone. In the presence of others he was stiff, stilted, and cold, but out alone in the night, in the wilderness, he was strictly a killer.

A solitary man by disposition, he had much in his nature to make others uncomfortable. Faultlessly neat, he wore the plainest of clothes, always carefully brushed. His thin hair was combed close to his scalp; his jaws were never unshaven. He had never been seen to tip back in a chair, lean against a wall or a post, or to make any careless gesture.

None of the Munson riders were at all unhappy he chose to remain behind and follow along later. His pres-

ence put a damper on idle talk, and it was well known
that he disliked profane or obscene language. His
standards and morals were largely those of the hard-
shell Baptist family in which he had grown up, and had
he discarded his guns there was nothing in his conduct
to which they could have objected. He was a man with a
single, deadly vice.

The usual conceptions of fair play were foreign to
him. He killed his enemies when and where he found
them, and at his own convenience. He wasted no efforts,
and wasted no lead. He disliked gun battles in streets or
saloons, avoided any display of temper on the part of
others, and showed no emotions of his own. His peculiar
walk and his high-shouldered, erect bearing drew attention; otherwise he was colorless.

His mother had been a Munson, an Alabama cousin
of the Texas family. The Texas family had, several
generations back, migrated from Germany to Mexico,
and had moved to Texas some years later. Jackson
Huddy heard of the Munson-Kittery feud in Missouri,
and rode south to help his family. The first Kittery he
killed was a pleasant young man, Al Kittery, who rode
in from El Paso to visit his kin. He commented, in a saloon, that it looked as if the family might need his help.

When Al Kittery left the saloon and went into the
street, Jackson Huddy followed.

Al Kittery, it had been said, was quite a hand with
a gun, but he had not killed anyone. Loafers in the
saloon heard two shots that sounded almost as one,
and going out, they found Al Kittery's hand on his
half-drawn gun and two bullet holes in his heart. Jackson Huddy was gone.

Now, standing on the street in Indianola, Huddy
watched the stage arrive. He was waiting for Every
Munson, the only one of the family to whom he was in
any way close. Ev Munson was as completely opposite in appearance to Huddy as a man could be—young,
handsome, reckless of bearing, inclined to the flam-
boyant in dress and manner. Only in one thing were they

alike, for when it came to killing, Ev was as cool and efficient as Huddy himself.

Every Munson would not be on the stage, but he would be riding up that same street within minutes, if he was on time, and he usually was. This was another reason Jackson Huddy had let the others ride on ahead . . . he wanted to see Ev without the others.

The stage rolled in and came to a stop; the dust cloud that trailed behind it caught up and settled over and around the stage. The first man out was a fat drummer, his vest buttons spread so wide over his stomach that glimpses of white shirt showed between them.

The second person to get down was a young woman, and when the drummer turned and held out his hand to help her, she took it and stepped lightly into the street, and all Indianola stopped in its stride.

Jessica Trescott, of the Virginia and New York Trescotts, stepped down onto dusty Main Street of Indianola and looked about her, in no way disturbed by the shabby little western town. She had dignity as well as elegance and charm, and no amount of heat, dust, or travel could wilt any of it.

There were a dozen women along the street, and each paused, some of them peeking around parasols, some frankly staring, for Jessica's clothes had come from Paris. Not Paris of last year or two years ago, but the Paris of today, almost of tomorrow. She wore an all-beige dress with black pleated ruching at the hem, on the caught-up apron part, and the tight-waisted jacket. The straw hat was worn well back on the coiffure which was done with a chignon. There was an embroidered veil and a small velvet bow on the hat.

That was the moment when Mady Coppinger rode up to the hitching rail and swung down. She turned, and found herself facing the vision of all she had ever wished to be, and she stared, resentfully admiring.

Jessica Trescott smiled. "How do you do? I am Jessica Trescott. That hotel over there . . . is it a good place? I mean a clean place, and a respectable one?"

"Yes, it is," Mady ansered. Then she added in a tone that sounded sullen, "I am Mady Coppinger."

"Mady—! But of course! You are Mr. Kittery's fiancée. Then maybe you can tell me where I can find Tappan Duvarney?"

Mady Coppinger's interest in the question did not seem very marked. "He's coming up the trail now," she said. "He should be in town before sunset."

"Do you know Tappan? I mean, if you know him—"

"I know him, and you can have him."

Jessica smiled again. "That's the general idea, Mady. Why else would I come here?"

"I can't imagine," Mady said, "why anybody would come here who could be anywhere else."

The porter from the hotel had crossed to pick up Jessica's carpetbag and small trunk. The men from the stage office were handing down still another trunk, and then a third.

"Are those all yours?" Mady asked.

"All mine. After all, you can't expect a girl to come unarmed and defenseless into a country like this, can you?" She turned to follow the porter. "Mady, I'm going to freshen up, and then I wish you'd join me—I am going to have tea, or something. Frankly, I'm famished!"

Then she was gone, leaving a faint scent of perfume behind her, and Mady looked after her enviously. Turning toward the boardwalk, she stopped abruptly. Ev Munson was standing there, grinning at her, his dark eyes dancing with amusement.

"That's quite a woman, Mady," he said; "quite a woman."

Mady replied sharply. "She's Tap Duvarney's girl, if you want to know. They're to be married."

He still grinned at her. "Young to be a widow," he said, "and she's goin' to be one before she's ever a wife!"

Mady stepped up on the boardwalk. "You got anything to tell me, Mady?" Ev Munson asked.

She hesitated, her eyes straying after Jessica, who had paused in the doorway to glance back. She made a move as if to draw away from Ev, then stopped. After all, Jessica had no idea who Ev was . . . what could it matter?

She stayed there, still looking across the street, standing near Ev but not seeming to be talking to him. "Duvarney's coming into town tonight," she said, ". . . with a herd."

"A herd?" Ev Munson was incredulous. "They're makin' their gather down to Horseshoe Lake. We already seen them. Our boys are on their way down."

"Have it your way, but you be around tonight and you'll see the herd come in. This is just a part of it that Duvarney brought over from Matagorda Island."

"How many's with him?"

"Three or four, I think. They're all strangers except Welt Spicer."

"Strangers?" There was disappointment in Ev's tone. "Are you sure?"

"Ev"—Mady looked around at him for the first time —"I want my money now."

"Money?" Ev said. "Now look, honey, you know damn well—"

"I want my money, Ev. You promised. You promised me two hundred dollars if I'd tell you where they all were and what they were doing. You promised me that two months ago."

"Sure, honey. Now you just wait—"

"I'm not waiting, Ev. I want my money, and I'm going to have it. I'm going to New Orleans."

He gave her a wicked smile. "Suppose you don't get it? You goin' to tell Tom on me? Or that Duvarney fella?"

"No, Ev." Her eyes sparked. "I'll tell Jackson Huddy!"

The taunting smile vanished. "You'll do nothin' of the kind, damn you! You'll—"

"I want my money, Ev," she repeated. "I want it

tomorrow. No," she said with sudden anger, "I want it tonight, and I want every last cent of it. What I've been doing is a pretty mean thing, but I need that money, and if I don't get it I'll go straight to Jackson Huddy and tell him. You know how he is about breaking your word; and above all, how he is about women. He'd kill you, Ev."

"Like hell!" Ev's eyes slanted up the street. "I think I could beat him, anyway. I'm faster than he is."

"Want me to tell him that too? Anyway, it doesn't matter how fast you are, he would kill you. He would kill you whenever he was of a mind to and you'd never know he'd done it."

Ev swore under his breath. "All right, I'll get your money. You just wait. I'll bring it by the ho-tel tonight."

She walked away, and Ev stood there staring along the street, eaten by anger and hatred. He had been top man among the Munsons, top man with a gun at least, until Jackson Huddy came along. Since then he had taken second place, and he did not like it. At the same time, Jackson Huddy was all that kept them going, for a good half of the Munsons wanted no part of the Kitterys. It was only the fact that Huddy would do most of the killing and take most of the risks that held them together.

Tom Kittery was supposed to be fast, but it was not Kittery who worried Ev Munson, it was Jackson Huddy. Huddy gave no man a fair chance, but Ev did not dare try to kill him, for without Huddy the Munsons would have to back up and sit down and shut up. Jackson Huddy's reputation and the fear that ringed around him gave them all a sort of courage.

Once in her room, Jessica did not take time to change. She freshened up a bit, brushed her hair, and replaced her hat. But she did take time to open her trunks and hang out some of her dresses to get the wrinkles out of them. She would have to see if she could hire somebody to do some pressing for her, and some laundry. If not, she would do it herself. She never had, but she could.

Thoughtfully, she considered Mady Coppinger. Why had she turned away so guiltily when Jessica saw her with that man? Because Jessica knew she was spoken for by Tom Kittery? Or was it something else?

She thought of how the man looked—dark, handsome in a tough, daring sort of way, but dirty, actually unclean. He had passed near her and she had seen the collar of his shirt was shiny with dirt. She shuddered. Her father had warned her that the world she was coming into was like nothing she had ever known. She had tried to learn about it, going more than once to the blacksmith down at the Corners, who had lived in Texas, and knew all about it. He came from Goliad, which was not far from this town. He had even known about the Kitterys and the Munsons. It was, he said, a bitterly fought feud.

Well, she would go to the dining room and eat . . . she had never been so hungry. After that she would return here and keep a watch out for Tap. She had forgotten to ask where he was coming from, but there were only two possible choices, unless he was planning to swim the cattle in. She smiled at that, for Tappan Duvarney was just the sort of man who might.

She thought again of the man Mady had spoken to . . . it was almost as if she did not want to be seen talking to him. Still, in such a country as this she must know all sorts of people. As far as that went, Jessica herself had known all kinds. The Judge, her father, had not exactly sheltered his only daughter. Since her mother died they had been very close, and she had often ridden into the country with him when he was buying stock or was riding to some other town to hold court.

She picked up her purse and left the room, and found her way to the dining room. She had been there only a few minutes when Mady Coppinger came in and joined her.

Mady looked across the table at her, enviously. "You look so . . . so *right*. I wish I could look like that."

"It isn't that difficult," Jessica said. "And why look as I do? You're beautiful enough as you are. Mr. Kittery must think so."

"Oh . . . *Tom*. Tom's all right—he's a grand fellow, but he doesn't have any ambition. He doesn't want to *go* anywhere."

"Go?"

"I mean he wants to stay here. In the West, that is. All he can think about is cattle. Sometimes I think that's all he knows."

"Maybe it is, but if he's a good man and he loves you . . . " Jessica paused. "And if you love him. You do, don't you?"

"I think so. I don't know. I just wish he'd take me away from here. I don't want to spend my life on a cattle ranch in Texas. Maybe . . . maybe if he loses out here he will go away. I mean if this deal falls through."

Jessica lifted her eyes slowly. "You mean his deal with Tappan? Do you think that will fail?"

"I don't know. It's just that it is such an awful gamble, driving cattle all that way. And if they do sell for a good price they will only buy more and do it all over again."

Jessica was thoughtful. She ordered a small meal, but most of all, she listened. She had heard discontented women before this, but never one who seemed quite so desperate. What it was Mady wanted from life Jessica could not decide; but whatever it was she did not expect to find it here. To her the "city"—a vague, rather unreal conception of the actual thing—was where she wished to be . . . and if Tom did not take her there she would go anyway . . . anyhow.

"How could he make a living there?" Jessica asked in a mild tone.

"Tom? Oh . . . oh, he'd find something. Men always do."

"It isn't that easy, I'm afraid. I mean without some special ability."

Mady refused to accept that. "He could find something. He just won't try."

"Why should he? He has a place here, people know him, respect him. He owns cattle. He owns land. If I were you I'd grab him quick. He sounds like a catch."

"Tom?" Mady was astonished. "He'll never be anything but a cattleman."

Jessica changed the subject then, talking lightly of other things—of the East and, although she disliked to mention such matters, of how much things cost in the cities. Mady's discontent was obvious, so what Jessica hoped to do was to indicate that the grass on the other side of the fence was no greener.

Finally, when Mady left her, Jessica relaxed and ordered coffee, genuinely relieved that the other girl had gone. From where she sat she could look out on the street, see the horses along the rail, and watch the people come and go along the boardwalk.

One of the men she saw was the man who had been talking earlier with Mady, and he was with a tall, austere-looking man. Once the latter caught her eyes upon him and he lifted his hat. The other man noticed and made some remark, at which his companion turned to look at her again with curious, penetrating attention.

"More coffee?" The waitress was at her side.

"Please. Most of the men out there . . . are they cattlemen?"

"Them? Loafers, most of them. There's some cattlemen, buyers, and a few shipping men. But mostly they're trash."

"The dark one with the red-topped boots—is he a cattleman?"

"You could call him that. He's one of that Munson outfit. You know, the ones that have the feud. They do run cattle, but they're usually too busy hunting Tom Kittery or boozing it up, to do any work."

"Munson? I've heard the name."

"That's Ev . . . he's ringleader since the old man was killed. Him and Jackson Huddy."

Jessica sat up a little straighter. What was Mady Coppinger, Tom Kittery's girl, doing talking to Ev Munson, a leader of the opposition? Jessica was young, but her years had been lived closer to the business and the courts of the land, so she was acquainted, at least by second-hand, with the perfidy of the world. If one thought of Mady's feverish desire to escape from Texas and the cattle range, and you coupled that with her whispering to Ev Munson . . .

Surely she was imagining things. Nevertheless, she was worried, and she remained by the window until the supper crowd started to gather. Then she went to her room, put on a black cloak, and went back down the stairs.

"Ma'am?" The clerk was a kindly, elderly man. "I'd not go out on that street if I were you. We've got good folks hereabouts, but there's riffraff too."

"Just for a breath of air. I won't leave the boardwalk."

She stepped outside. The wind off the Gulf was light and cool. The night was very still. Only a few stars were out, and a vague light lingered in the western sky.

At first she thought there was nobody on the street but herself, and then, not sixty feet away, she saw a tall, slender figure. It was that man with the odd, high-shouldered appearance, and he was coming toward her.

9

He stopped in front of her, not quite blocking her way, and when he spoke it was in an odd, almost hesitant way.

"Ma'am?" He cleared his throat. "I would not be out on the street if I were you. There . . . there is often trouble . . . rough men . . ." His voice trailed off, then seemed to gather power as he added, "Sometimes even shooting."

"Thank you. It was very close inside," she said quietly, and "I wanted a breath of air."

"Yes, it must be stuffy inside. I think there's . . ." He hesitated again. "I think there's a storm . . . ,change in the weather." He lifted his hat. "I am Jackson Huddy, ma'am. You take your walk, and if you are bothered . . . . if anyone stops you, tell them I am near."

"Thank you, Mr. Huddy."

He bowed and stepped aside, and she walked on. He had seemed embarrassed, almost frightened by her, and her curiosity was aroused. She remembered hearing the waitress mention Jackson Huddy as a man who was a leader among the Munsons.

Jackson Huddy and Ev Munson were in Indianola, and the herd was due to arrive tonight, she was thinking. Tappan Duvarney might be coming up that road at any time.

She walked on to the end of the street, then crossed over, holding her skirts up a little to keep them from the dust. Far down the street she could see Jackson Huddy, and she was about to start back when she heard the muffled footfalls of a horse walking in the dust.

She stood very still listening. There was more than one horse, and they were coming up an alleyway between the buildings. When they appeared at the edge of the line of buildings they drew rein, and she could see their heads thrust out to peer down the street.

Then one of them spoke. "Too quiet. I don't like it, Major."

"Where's the hotel where Brunswick will be staying?" It was Tappan's voice.

She stepped forward and said quietly, just loud enough for them to hear. "He is at my hotel, Tappan."

The heads jerked around, and Tap Duvarney said, "Jessica! Is that you, or am I going crazy?"

She walked toward them. "Yes, Tappan, I am here. . . . Be careful, Tappan. Huddy and Ev Munson are still in town, and they know you're bringing in some cattle."

"Now, how the dev—?" Tap began, then went on, "How did you know that?"

"I met Mady Coppinger, and she told me. I think she also told them. She was on the street, standing very close to Ev Munson, and I think she was whispering to him."

"How long have you been in town, Jessica?"

"Several hours," she said.

"And you know all that? And you know who Ev Munson is?"

She smiled brightly. "I also know who Jackson Huddy is, and if I don't keep moving he will be up here to see what's wrong. He told me that if anybody bothered me, to mention that he was near."

"Jackson Huddy?" Tap was incredulous.

"He's like that about womenfolks," Spicer said. "He's almighty respectful to them, and I think a mite scared of them."

"Do you want to see Mr. Brunswick?" Jessica asked. "I heard him named at the hotel, and if you want me to, I could speak to him and arrange it. When I came out he was reading a newspaper in the lobby."

"Could you do that? We'll be at the corral. No," Duvarney said, changing his mind. "Ask him to go to his room. I'll see him there. Welt, you and Bean stay off the streets."

"We'll wait in the barn, yonder. You watch your step, Major. That Jackson Huddy is pure poison, and Ev Munson is hell on wheels with a six-gun. He's killed eight or nine men I know of."

"Jessica, " Tap warned, "you be careful."

"You too. I can't wait to have a talk with you. Later, at the hotel?"

"If I can. This is touch and go."

She walked away, taking her time, and when she passed Jackson Huddy he looked at her, then looked away quickly.

"Good night, Mr. Huddy," she said. "And thank you."

"Yes—yes, ma'am." He spoke so quickly he almost stuttered.

When Jessica got back to the hotel, Bob Brunswick was no longer in the lobby. She stopped at the desk to get her key, and as the clerk was not around, she glanced at the register. Brunswick was only three rooms down the hall from her own. She went up the stairs, opened the door of her room, and put down her key. Then she walked down the hall and tapped lightly on Brunswick's door. He opened it slightly, then wider.

He was a large, portly man with a black walrus mustache. He was in his shirtsleeves; a heavy gold watch-chain with an elk's tooth was draped across his stomach. His expression now was startled.

"Mr. Brunswick? I am Jessica Trescott, and I would like to speak to you." She smiled slightly. "I am a lady, Mr. Brunswick."

He flushed. "I can see that, ma'am. The lobby, then?"

"No, it must be here ... now ... and quickly."

He stepped back, and when she had entered he closed the door. Taking his coat from the back of a chair, he put it on. "Sorry, ma'am, for the cigar smoke. I wasn't expecting a lady."

"Mr. Brunswick, you are a cattle buyer. My fiancé, Mr. Tappan Duvarney, is right down the street. He is bringing in a herd, and they will arrive very soon, I believe. Jackson Huddy and Ev Munson are on the street too, and Tappan does not want trouble. He wanted me to ask you to stay in your room and wait for him."

"Whose cattle are they?"

"He is in partnership with Tom Kittery, who is, I believe, holding another herd somewhere south of here."

"All right, I'll wait." He took up his cigar, started to smoke, then rubbed it out. "Ma'am ... Miss Trescott, if I were you and I loved that man I'd get him out of here—fast."

She smiled. "Mr. Brunswick, you would do no such a thing ... not if you were me. Tappan is a man, doing a man's work. It is the work he chose to do, and I would never interfere. As for danger, I suspect there are many men in danger right now, in a lot of ways. I might tell you something about Tappan, Mr. Brunswick.

"He is not a man I could persuade to leave here; and if I could, I wouldn't want him. Nor is he a man to be intimidated. Major Tappan Duvarney," she said, lifting her chin a little, "is a veteran soldier, sir. He has been in campaigns against the Kiowas, the Apaches, the

Sioux, the Cheyennes and the Modocs. Also, there was a western town, Mr. Brunswick, with a very bad reputation, which was near Tappan's post, and he was deputized to clean it up. He did so, Mr. Brunswick, in just three days. I believe there were several altercations."

Brunswick smiled warmly. "Ma'am, whoever he is, he must be quite a man to deserve you. I'll wait for him, right here." He opened the door. "And you know something? I'm not going to worry about him—not a bit."

Jessica went back to her room and removed her hat. She sat down in the rocker, but she could not remain still. Tappan was out there in the night . . . and he was in danger.

She should, she decided, be frightened. Yet she was not. Always when traveling with her father she had a feeling of being a bystander, of observing the courts in action, of witnessing violence after the fact. She had always had more confidence than other girls, always was more assured. Now, instead of being depressed by the impending danger, she felt exhilarated. She was frightened, yes, and she was worried. Part of her mind admitted this, but the other part was enjoying the sense of being part of things.

She knew exactly why she had come to Texas. She had faced her father with it several times in the weeks before she left. Tappan Duvarney was, she said, the only man she had ever wanted to marry; but Tappan was fiercely proud, fiercely independent. It would be just like him not to come back if things did not go well for him, and she had no idea of taking that risk.

"I'm going after him, Father, I'm going to Texas," she had said.

Some fathers would have been furious, some would have refused to permit any such thing. Hers was amused, and interested.

Judge Trescott had enjoyed the company of his daughter for longer than he had expected, and he had watched her grow and develop in personality and character. She was much like her mother, even more like himself, and she was somewhat like her grandmother on his side. But most of all, she was somebody new; she was herself.

He had not done as much for her as he would have liked, but he had tried to offer a guiding hand, and friendly advice. Youngsters invariably began by thinking their parents were "old-fashioned," "out of date," or "back numbers," and they usually ended by admitting how right the parents had been, in most cases.

Jessica had traveled with him, had taken care of him, scolded him, admired him, and had been not only his daughter but his friend. But until Major Tappan Duvarney came along he had seen no one he thought worthy of her. He had admitted none of this to her, merely watching from the sidelines. He knew that a lot of the old ladies, both male and female, had deplored his taking his growing daughter around the country with him, and had been shocked at his permitting her to sit in the courtroom while he tried his cases. Many of these were civil cases, but many were criminal, so that Jessica at nineteen had few illusions about the kind of people there were in the world, and about the situations with which she might be faced.

He had listened to her talk of Tappan Duvarney and he was pleased with his daughter. He agreed that Tap was just the sort to remain away if he did not at first succeed.

"All right," he said, "if you love Tap, go get him." He smiled at her.

Then, just as she was packing he had come into her room carrying a pistol. It was a Colt five-shot, .41 caliber House Pistol. "Put this in your things," he said, and with it he gave her a small sack. "There are fifty rounds there. If you need more," he said with a smile, "you'd better get a bigger gun."

Her eyes met his. "Do you think I'll need that, Father?"

"I doubt it, but let's say it is insurance. Texas is a country where they respect women, but I can't promise that you'll always find it so."

She went to her carpetbag now and removed the pistol, which was loaded. The barrel was short; the pistol would fit into her handbag. Heavy, yes, but reassuring in its weight.

The dining room was open until ten o'clock. In a few minutes she would go down, eat a leisurely supper, and listen to what was happening. She tried to read . . . but a part of her mind was alert to the outside sounds. She knew what she listened for, what she expected and feared—pistol shots.

Tappan Duvarney stood at the opening between the buildings and surveyed the street. Far down, he could see the tall, dark figure of a man. Other men were walking along the street, and occasionally one disappeared into or emerged from a saloon. There were lights along the street; a few horses were tied to the hitching rails, with here and there a buckboard. At this hour no wagons were in sight.

Tap stepped out and walked down to the hotel and entered. The clerk looked up and Duvarney asked for Brunswick's room, and disappeared up the steps. The clerk looked up after him, then glanced nervously at the door. He did not know Tappan Duvarney by sight, but he had heard him described, and this stranger looked like the description.

Tap knocked lightly on the door, and Brunswick opened it, glanced at him, and stepped back. "Come in," he said. "You have cattle to sell? How many?"

"At a rough count, I'd say eight hundred and thirty head."

"What kind of shape are they in?"

"You've seen island cattle. This is a mixed lot, mostly big stuff, and they're in good shape. I'd say about half of them are steers upwards of five years old."

Brunswick chewed his cigar. "Those cattle on the island are usually in good shape—lots of feed, and they don't have to go far to water; but beef prices aren't at their best now."

"I want a fast deal," Tap said quietly, "and I've heard you're a fair man."

Brunswick rolled his cigar in his lips. "I've got to ship to New Orleans. There'll be some loss at sea." He took a good look at Tap, and said, "I'll give you twelve dollars a head, right across the board."

"Twelve dollars? Brunswick, there's some steers in that lot who'll weigh fifteen hundred pounds."

"Sure there are. And there's probably forty, fifty head in there won't weigh more than a hundred pounds. That's mixed stuff."

"Make it sixteen?"

Bob Brunswick shrugged. "Fourteen; and I'll be lucky not to take a loss."

"All right, I'll go along. You make the check for eight hundred head. If there's less, I'll make it up, and if there's more—and there is—you can have them."

Brunswick sat down at the table and wrote the check and handed it to Duvarney. "There you are, Tap, and my regards to the little lady. She's got sand, that girl."

"Thanks." Duvarney hesitated. "Brunswick, you've been fair, so I'll give you a piece of advice. Either get those cattle loaded and out to sea, or drive them inland —ten miles inland."

Brunswick took the cigar from his mouth. "What are you telling me?"

"That's hurricane weather out there. I can smell it."

"All right." He paused. "Duvarney, your boys are moving those cattle. What do you say if you keep right on moving them? Start them toward Victoria, and hold them somewhere along Placedo Creek."

Tap considered. He had hoped to get his men right

out of town to avoid trouble, yet he could scarcely leave Brunswick in the lurch, and finding cowhands at this hour of the night, or even tomorrow, would be difficult. Yet this might be the very best way . . . or it might be the worst.

"I could hold them here," Brunswick said. "If I get them penned up they can't stampede."

"Have you ever seen a hurricane, Brunswick? I was a seaman in the West Indies and along the Atlantic coast for several years. This storm started some place far south of Cuba, maybe off the coast of Brazil, and she's been moving north. Those winds will be blowing hard enough to flatten anything around here, but the whole storm won't move more than fifteen miles an hour."

"That doesn't make sense."

"The winds blow in a big circle, ten or twenty miles across. I don't know that anybody ever measured one, but I'd guess a couple I ran into were that big."

Tap paused. "I'd move them," he said again. "Somewhere back on the prairie, this side of Victoria."

"They'd have to go right through town. Have you ever seen cattle go through a town?"

"They're tired. I think they'd handle easy. You want to try it?"

"Well . . . you've got my money. You made your deal. You've no reason to stay on unless you want to."

"I've already agreed. You pay the boys what you think the job is worth." He pocketed the check. "Let's go, then."

"You'd better see that little lady before you go. She's worried."

Tap opened the door and glanced up and down the hall, then he stepped out. Almost at once, Jessica's door opened.

"Tap . . . oh, Tap!" He went to her, caught her hands.

"You shouldn't have come here," he said. "But now that you have come, you should get out. There's going to be a storm."

"You go on. I'll be all right."

She listened while he explained about moving the cattle. "If the storm looks bad, I'll come back for you, but don't wait here for me. If it starts to blow up, go to the courthouse. It's on a knoll in the center of town, and the building is solid. If anything in town comes through all right, the courthouse will."

"Don't worry," she said. "I'll be all right."

He went down the stairs and walked across the lighted lobby. Stepping out onto the walk, he came face to face with a tall, lean man.

It was Jackson Huddy.

10

In western towns where the work begins at daybreak or earlier, supper is eaten early, and most good citizens are in bed before ten o'clock. It is only along the main streets where the saloons and the honky-tonks are that people drink and gamble far into the night.

Indianola was in bed or preparing for it. The night was still and the air seemed close; there was something in the atmosphere that made animals restless and men irritable. There lay over the town and the flatlands beyond a breathless hush that seemed like a warning.

The truth of the matter was that Indianola had not long to live. Here, within the space of a few hours, a town was to be destroyed, a way of living wiped out. And nobody was aware of it.

Down along the two piers that thrust their long fingers into the bay waters, the masters of the few ships in port were nevously running out additional lines. The swell breaking on Matagorda Island had already become so great that getting through the channel would be a doubtful matter . . . nobody wanted to try it. And few seaports anywhere seemed more sheltered than Indianola.

When Tappan Duvarney stepped out on the street and came face to face with Jackson Huddy there was a moment when neither man moved nor spoke. Then Jackson Huddy said, "You are driving Rafter K cattle."

"Some are Rafter K, some wear my own brand, but I am a businessman, Mr. Huddy, doing business in cattle. I have no interest in the Munson-Kittery feud, as I have said before this."

"How long before you'll be drawn in?" Huddy asked.

"That depends on the Munsons. If they move against me or my men, they must accept the consequences. If they do not move against us, they have nothing to fear."

"We do not fear, Major Duvarney."

"Do not disregard fear, Mr. Huddy. A little fear inspires caution. I have learned there is a little fear and a little caution in every victory. And from what I have heard of you, I had suspected you to be a cautious man."

"And what have you heard of me?" The small blue eyes were probing, curious, yet somehow they were strangely empty.

"That you take no unnecessary chances; that to you victory is the result to be desired, and the method is less important."

"You do not like that?"

Duvarney smiled. "Mr. Huddy, I cut my eyeteeth on the Apaches, the greatest guerilla fighters the world has ever seen, and I have had some dealings with the Sioux and the Cheyennes too. I found their methods very useful to me, and easily understood. As in all things, Mr. Huddy, the number of possibilities of attack is limited. One considers those that are manifestly impossible. They are eliminated, and the others prepared for. We killed or captured a lot of Apaches."

"Is that a threat?"

Duvarney did not answer the question, but said, "Mr. Huddy, you have a certain reputation. Why risk it against a man who is not your enemy?"

Deliberately, he walked past him and on down the street, moving easily, stepping lightly, ready to throw himself to right or left if the need arose, and picking one vantage point after another as he walked along. He had no idea that what he had said would matter in the long run, for Jackson Huddy would move as the situation seemed to dictate; yet he had to say what he could in an effort to prevent a gun battle that could kill good men and serve no one.

Doc Belden had reached the rendezvous point. The cattle were still moving, however. Tap rode out to swing alongside of him, riding point.

"I've sold the cattle," he said to Belden, "and we're going inland, away from the storm. We're taking them right down the main street."

"You're taking a chance. If they stampede in town they could bust up a lot of stuff."

"They're tired," Tap said. "Also, I think they're ready to turn away from the sea. There's a storm coming."

He paused, then added, "Pass the word along. Every man is to ride with the thong off his pistol. He must be ready to fight, if need be."

In the southeast the stars were gone, and the night sky showed a bulging, billowing mass of cloud that seemed to heave itself higher and higher against the sky as the moments passed. The cattle broke into a half-trot, settled back into a walk, and then began to trot again. Belden and Tap swung the point into the street.

At the muffled thunder of hoofs, lights suddenly blazed and doors opened. A murmur, then a growl ran along the street, but though the cattle were tired, they were intent on moving, and they went silently, except for the beat of their hoofs in the dust, and the rustle of their sides against one another. Here and there horns clacked against each other; a cowboy, moving up on some recalcitrant steer, called "Ho!" They moved steadily on, keeping to the street.

The people, watching, became silent. A few came out on the boardwalk to look at the sky when there was a far-off rumble of thunder.

A gust of wind blew along the street, creaking signs, rattling shutters. A brief spatter of rain fell, then subsided. The night was perfectly still.

The last of the cattle passed, and they vanished up the street.

Jessica, standing in the dark by her window watching the street below, breathed softly in relief, scarcely believing it had been done. Then a door nearby opened and a tall man came out on the street, and she saw that it was Jackson Huddy. He was followed by another, a man with a slouching, lazily affected walk, who leaned against a post by the boardwalk and stood there with thumbs behind his belt. Out of the night two other men came up the street and joined them.

Her light was out, her curtain unmoving, but Jackson Huddy twice turned his head to look up as if he felt the impact of her eyes. No matter what they planned, there was nothing she could do now—she could only wait.

And then the wind came.

It began with a wall-shuddering blast, and a quick spatter of rain. Jessica opened her window and pulled the shutters together and fastened them. She could hear others doing the same, and through a crack in the shutters she could see men on the street in their nightshirts or in hastily donned Levis putting up shutters, and in some cases nailing them down.

She had not undressed, and suddenly she decided she would not.

The old building creaked under the weight of the wind, and somewhere something slammed against a building and fell heavily against the boardwalk—probably one of the street signs. Looking through the cracks in the shutters, she could no longer see any lights, and suddenly she realized it was because of fear of fire.

Outside, lightning now flashed almost continuously, lighting the sky weirdly. The bulging clouds were lower than she had ever seen clouds before. She was frightened, and she admitted that to herself. But she remained calm, considering the situation.

Nothing can be done about a storm. One takes what precautions one can, and then waits. Now Jessica lighted her lamp and placed it, turned low, on the floor, so that it could not be knocked from the table. Propping her pillows against the base of the bed, she got out a book of poetry and sat down to read, but after a minute she gave up. The roar of the wind was now terrific.

Suddenly someone banged on her door and she went over to it, hesitating only a moment, to be sure she had the gun. Holding it in the folds of her skirt, she opened the door.

Mady Coppinger stood there, soaked to the skin, gasping for breath, and wild with fear.

"Please! Let me come in!"

Jessica stepped back, and when Mady was inside, she closed the door and stood with her back against it.

"Oh, I hope you'll forgive me, but I had no place else to go!" Mady's voice shook. "It's awful out there—awful!"

"You must get out of those clothes," Jessica said practically. "I have some dry things you can wear."

Mady sat down, trembling. Her shoes and ankles were muddy, and she herself was literally drenched. Her hair had come undone and hung about her face and shoulders.

Jessica asked no questions, offered no comment. She gave Mady towels, and when it did not appear that those she had would be adequate, she went across the hall to an empty room and took the towels she found there.

Slowly Mady began to calm down. "It's awful out there," she repeated, almost to herself. "I've never seen anything like this."

"You'd better change. We may have to leave the hotel. Tappan said we should go to the courthouse."

"It's on higher ground," Mady said. "Yes, I think we'd better."

She dressed hurriedly, but as she did so she was admiring the clothes she was putting on.

Jessica listened to the wind. She went to the closet and took out her warmest coats, a mackintosh and an ulster. The mackintosh was rain-proof, or close to it; the ulster was heavier, and warm. She was trying to decide, even as she took down the coats, what was the best thing to do. Tappan's advice was clear in her mind, but wouldn't they say she was just a silly woman? And suppose the courthouse was closed?

It was raining now, if one could call it that: a tremendous sheet of water was smashing down the narrow street, and she could feel the weight of it against the wall of the building. Even as she put on the mackintosh and prepared to leave the room, one part of her mind was wondering where Mady Coppinger had been and what she had been doing on such a night. . . . And had her terror been only the terror of the storm?

They went down the stairs, feeling the straining of the building, and into the lobby. They found themselves in a tight group of people. A few were whimpering in fear, but most were silent, listening to the terrible sound outside, hearing the thunder of the storm.

Jessica pushed her way through them and they gave way, staring at her blankly.

Near the door she saw the clerk standing with Mr. Brunswick and two other men, both of whom were solid-seeming men, those who are among the leaders in any community.

"Mr. Brunswick?" He turned impatiently, then removed his hat. "Mr. Brunswick, can you let us out?" Jessica said.

"In this? Ma'am, I wouldn't let anybody out in a storm like this. There's water almost knee-deep in the streets right now."

"Tappan . . . Major Duvarney . . . advised me to take shelter in the courthouse if the storm got worse. I believe we should go while we can."

"What's Duvarney know about storms?" The speaker was an austere-looking man with a permanently disagreeable expression.

"Major Duvarney was a seafaring man before he went into the army," Jessica replied stiffly. "He was an officer on ships in the West Indian trade. He knows the sea, and he knows hurricanes."

Worriedly, the gray-haired man beside Brunswick asked, "Did he think this was going to be a hurricane?"

"He told me there had been great swells breaking on Matagorda Island for several days, and such swells come only from a great storm at sea." While she answered him her eyes looked at the street.

Through the front windows, where some of the shutters had been blown away, she could see outside. The water was surging out there, and it was deep. Signs were down, and there was a scattering of debris lying across the walks. Even as she looked, some flying shingles whipped past the window.

"I've never seen it this bad," Mady said.

The thirty or more people gathered in the lobby were staring at the storm. Only a few of them were dressed for what must lie ahead.

"All right," Brunswick said, "we'll try it. We'll have to stay close to the buildings where we can, and hang onto each other."

Suddenly there was a tremendous blast of wind that ripped the few remaining signs from the buildings along the street, and sailed them before it. At the same moment a great rush of water tore by, ripping up a part of the boardwalk and filling the street with a deeper rushing torrent.

Now all lights were out. The town stood in darkness,

all sound drowned out by the whistling roar of the
hurricane. Somewhere a sound did break through, a
sound of splintering wood; and then the wall of a building hurtled past. The corner hit the door of the hotel
and smashed a panel before the force of the water
tore it free and sent it on.

"We'll never make it now," the gray-haired man said
solemnly.

"We can make it, Crain," Brunswick replied. "Let's
wait until this spell is over."

"If it ever is," Mady said.

Jessica was silent, thinking about Tappan. He was out
there somewhere in that roaring world of wind and
water. He was out there moving cattle in all this . . .
or he was dead.

It was ten o'clock at night when the storm first came
to Indianola, and by the time the full force of the wind
was beginning to smash the town Tap Duvarney had
his cattle several miles west of the town and was driving
them hard.

To the east, out over the Gulf, lightning flashed in-
termittently, showing great masses of wind-torn clouds.

From out of the night, violence and the storm, and
the vast thunder that rolled on and on, each enormous
crash followed by another. From out of the night a
moving wall of slashing rain, a wall of steel. The roof of
clouds seemed only a few feet above the heads of the
frightened cattle and the straining riders.

Tap Duvarney had turned to look back, and was
appalled. He could see the storm coming upon them.
At the bottom it was a ragged cloud and the steel mesh
of the rain; above, the massed black clouds were laced
with lightning.

"Look, Doc," he said. "Look at that and you can tell
them you've seen hell with the doors open."

Belden's face was pale. "What do we do?" he asked.

"Try to hold them in a bunch. That's all we can do.
It can't last forever."

Lawton Bean pulled up alongside them, his face strangely yellowish in the odd light. "I wonder what's happening back there in town," he said. "One time when I was a kid I lived on Matagorda. I seen the sea break clean over the island. Dad and me, we made a run for it."

"You made it, looks like," Belden said.

"I did ... pa didn't."

Hunched in their slickers, they watched the backs of the cattle as seen in the flashes of lightning. The rain hammered on the animals until they were almost numb from the beating.

"We've got to get shelter," Tap called out. "Keep your eyes out for a good bank that will keep us out of the wind!"

They had been moving steadily with the cattle at a trot a good part of the time. Tap thought for a moment of Lavaca Bay, which lay somewhere to the east ... but that would be too close to the path of the storm. He yelled at Belden and Bean, then started along the flank of the herd. At the point, with steady pressure, yells, and lashes with coiled lariats, they edged the herd to the west.

The cattle needed no urging, seeming to realize that the storm was behind them, and that safety, if there was any, would lie somewhere in the darkness ahead.

Slowly, the riders bunched. Welt Spicer came around the drag to join them, followed by Jule Simms.

"You seen Lon Porter?" Simms asked.

"Lon? He's over with Foster," Belden replied. "Or should be."

"Well, he ain't. He come up to me just as we were headin' into town. Had a message for the Major."

"I didn't see him." Tap Duvarney edged over toward Simms. "Did he say what he wanted?"

"He was huntin' you. Seems they had no trouble with the cattle ... most of them were already moving off the peninsula ... just like they knew this storm was headin' in. Lon told us that, then took off for town, a-huntin' you."

They were bunched now in the doubtful lee of a cluster of cottonwoods, and for a moment there seemed a lull in the storm.

"The feelin' I got," Simms said, "was there'd been trouble below . . . some shootin', more'n likely."

Why hadn't Lon Porter found him, Tap wondered. He had been in the hotel or on the street much of the time, and it would not have been difficult to locate him.

They rode on after the cattle, closing in around them, keeping them bunched, until in the gray light of a rain-lashed dawn they circled them at last on a small piece of prairie shielded by brush, mostly curly mesquite and tall-growing clusters of prickly pear. Here and there were a few small clumps of stunted post oak or hickory.

The exhausted cattle seemed to have no desire to go further, and they scattered out, some seeking shelter in the brush, but most of them simply dropping in their tracks. A few tried aimless bites at the coarse bunch grass, ignoring the sheets of rain and the wind. One clump of the mesquite and post oak had made a cove of shelter against the wind, and the riders rode in and dismounted.

Under the thickest of the brush they found a few leaves that were still dry, and they gathered some dead mesquite. After a brief struggle they had a fire going, half protected by a ground sheet stretched above it.

Jule Simms came up with a coffeepot, and soon there was water boiling. Lawton Bean, a limp cigarette trailing from his lips, hunched close to the small fire, nursing it with sticks. It gave off only a little heat, but it was comforting to see. The riders sat about, hunched in their slickers, staring dismally into the fire.

"How far did we come?" one of the men asked.

"Maybe twenty miles," Belden said. "We've been

moving seven or eight hours, and faster than any trail herd ought to travel under ordinary conditions."

Tap got up and rustled around in the brush, where he found an old mesquite stump that he worried from the muddy ground, then some dead mesquite branches and a fallen oak limb. He brought them back to the fire and started breaking them up.

"Lon was a good man," Lawton Bean said suddenly. "He was a mighty good man. I crossed the Rio Grande with him a couple of times, chasin' cow thieves."

"You think he's dead?" Tap asked.

"Well . . . look at it. You surely weren't hard to find in that piddlin' town, but he never showed up. He didn't have much of a ride to where you were, and he was hale an' hearty when he left us. I figure somebody killed him."

"If anybody killed Lon," Simms said quietly, "he's got me to answer to."

Lon might simply have got tired of the rain and taken shelter in a saloon. Yet he had a message so important he had ridden some miles to deliver it. To give up was not like Porter, and he was too recently from the army not to pay attention to duty.

"What do we do now?" Doc asked.

"You hole up and wait out the storm," Tap answered. "It's no use trying to push on in this. We've come to higher ground—"

"Not much higher," Bean interrupted.

"Probably thirty or forty feet higher," Tap said, "and we've come inland a good piece. We'll hold them here and keep a sharp lookout for Munsons. We're not out of the woods yet."

"You think they killed Lon?"

"Who knows? I agree that he could have found me easily enough. The way I see it, he would ride to the stockyards, and if he didn't find me there he'd come on up the street. I'm going to look around the yards for him first."

They stared at him then. "You goin' *back?*" Spicer said. "You're foolin'!"

"Lon was riding for me. I want to find him, or find out what happened to him. I want no part of this Munson feud, but if they've killed a man of mine, that's something I'll take care of."

"I'll go along with that." Doc Belden got up. "All right, if you're going, let's go."

"I'll go alone."

"Now, that's foolhardy," Spicer said. "If anybody goes it should be me. I know them boys, every last one of them."

Tap did not move, but stared at the fire, considering the situation. "If Lon came running for me in this weather," he said after a moment, "there was trouble, real trouble. So you better keep a sharp lookout."

"You think the Munsons would move with it blowing like this?"

"Most of them wouldn't. They'd be more likely to sit it out in comfort, but that isn't Jackson Huddy's way. It would be like him to use this storm to end the feud once and for all. You see, because of the drive he's got all the Kittery outfit bunched up where he wants them."

Still Tap lingered. He was no more anxious than any other man to leave even the small comfort of that fire for the storm outside. He looked around at the campsite. It was almost surrounded by the wall of mesquite, prickly pear, and post oak, but on one side it opened on the small parklike area where the cattle slept. Seeking shelter from the storm, they had also found a position that could be defended if necessary.

It was a dawn of rain and dark clouds, so low they seemed scarcely higher than the brush, and above all was the sound of the roaring wind. There was no question of escaping the rain; one could only hope to avoid the worst of it. The wind drove through the brush, bending the stiff branches, bending even the stunted trees until it seemed they must break or be uprooted.

They huddled together a minute or two longer. "You watch yourself, Major," Belden said quietly. "This here is one helluva storm. I never saw its like."

Tap wiped the water from the horse's back, then saddled it once more. Welt Spicer came up, a small bit of rawhide tied over the muzzle of his rifle.

There was a minute or two when the horses fought against facing the wind; then reluctantly they started, bending their heads low, pushing against it, moving forward with straining muscles.

11

Dawn came to Indianola with a weird yellow light, revealing the gray faces of the rain-hammered buildings, the dark, swirling water, ugly with foam and debris, rushing through the street. A lone steer, moss trailing from one great horn, came plunging and swimming along, a straggler from the herd, following blindly.

Somewhere up the street there was a crash as a wall gave way . . . more wreckage went by.

Jessica had risen from her seat in the old leather arm chair. "Mr. Brunswick," she said, "we've got to chance it. I think everything is going to go."

Reluctantly, he agreed. "All right." He looked around at the stunned, frightened people in the room. "We've got to get what blankets we can, and whatever food there is. There's no telling how long we'll be caught there."

"Major Duvarney will return," Jessica said. "He knows I am here."

"If he can," Brunswick responded grimly.

"Oh, no!" The words came from Mady in a low,

tortured cry. Jessica looked out at the water. Something else was swirling there, hanging for a moment against the smashed boards of the walk. It was a body, the body of a man, and it needed only a glimpse to see that no flood waters had killed this man. He had been shot . . . shot in the back of the head, and one side of his head was blown away.

For an instant nobody moved, then Brunswick and Crain lunged for the door, catching the body before it could be washed away, and getting it onto the solid part of the walk. Huddled over the body, they searched it for clues, and then stumbled back inside, Brunswick holding a small handful of money, some water-soaked papers, and a gun belt.

"His family might need this money," Brunswick said. He straightened the papers. One was an envelope addressed to Lon Porter, in care of a hotel at Brownsville, Texas. "Don't know him," he muttered.

"That man was murdered," Crain said sternly. "He was shot in the back of the head, at close range."

"There's twenty-six dollars here," Brunswick said. "Ma'am, will you see that this gets to whoever should have it? This letter here—I think you can make it out . . . that might help some."

"Yes." She took the money and the letter. She was thinking that this might be one of the men Tappan had hired. Brownsville . . . Fort Brown . . . yes, she was sure of it.

Something else occurred to her.

Mady . . . Mady had come to her room drenched to the skin and frightened, and there had been mud on her shoes. That was easy enough to get, even by crossing the street, but it had looked like the dirt from a stable or a corral. And Mady's sudden exclamation just now . . . was it only at seeing a man's dead body? Or was it because it was this particular man?

Jessica turned to look, but Mady had withdrawn and was working her way toward the back of the group, as if to avoid the accusing face of the dead man.

Jessica suddenly remembered their critical situation. "Mr. Brunswick," she said, "we've got to go. We've got to move right away."

Crain suddenly spoke up. "My God! We have prisoners locked in the jail!"

"Bill Taylor's in there," somebody said.

Just then two riders turned into the street, their horses almost belly-deep in the rolling water. Both men were bundled in slickers, and both had their hats tied under their chins, but she recognized Tappan at once.

She stepped to the door and Brunswick tried to restrain her. "Wait! We'll join hands! We can make a human chain, and the first ones who get to the courthouse can help the others."

"We'll have help," Jessica said. "There's Tappan Duvarney."

He rode up, facing his horse into the current. He saw her, started to speak, and then he saw the body of Lon Porter.

Instantly he swung to the hotel porch, which tilted badly under his weight, water sloshing over it. He bent over the body, turning the injured head gently with his fingers. Then he looked up. "Did anybody see this happen? Who shot him?"

Nobody answered, but involuntarily Jessica looked at Mady, whose face was taut and pale. Mady's stare was defiant, but she said nothing.

"His body floated down here," Brunswick said. "He must have been shot somewhere east of town."

"He was looking for me," Duvarney responded. "Somebody did not want him to see me, or else killed him because he was herding Rafter K cattle."

"We were going to make a try for the courthouse," Crain said. "I've got to go to the jail. If you could—"

Tap stepped back into the saddle and took down his rope. He shook it out. "Grab hold," he said, "and hang on."

People rushed to catch the rope, but Welt Spicer was

doing the same thing. Just then four riders turned into the upper end of the street.

"Look out, Major!" Spicer spoke quickly in a low tone. "Those are Munsons."

"Let's go!" Duvarney shouted to the crowd. "Let's go and keep moving!"

Crain, also mounted, was riding toward the jail. Tap caught a glimpse of him, and then could pay no more attention, for he needed every bit of his awareness. His horse started well, but the footing was bad; once the horse slipped, going almost to his knees, and it was only Tap's strength on the reins that pulled him up.

Half the people clinging to the rope were elderly. The wisest ones had managed to take a turn of the rope around their arms, for even if it was pulled taut and caused pain, it would at least hold them.

Only two persons were still at the hotel when Tap looked back. One was Bob Brunswick, and the other was Jessica. He almost pulled up when he saw her there, but she waved him on, and he lifted a hand and then spoke to his horse. "Steady, boy," he said. "Steady now."

A barn door went swinging by, narrowly missing the horse's legs. Tap squinted his eyes against the rain and stared ahead. At the corner, where two currents met, there was a swirling whirlpool. Somewhere along here the street was lower than further back . . . but where?

The four riders were coming nearer. He reached back and under the guise of straightening the rope, slid the thong from his pistol butt.

He felt the drive of the rain, and knew the sea was rising, rising with the wind. He looked back along the black swirling river of the street, and saw the collapsed buildings, the gutted stores, all torn and spoiled by sea and wind. His hat brim flapped against his brow; the wind tugged at the drawstring that held his hat in place, and flapped his slicker against the flanks of the horse.

"Steady, boy. Take it easy now."

The rocks that had washed from the makeshift

foundations were slippery, mud coated, and mud was deep in the street. He held to the side of the street for doubtful shelter from the wind. Always his eyes looked ahead, watching the wreckage as it hit the whirlpool at the corner, studying the currents, to move with them when crossing.

Actually, he was only supposed to be guiding the people, giving them something to cling to, but in effect he was hauling them along through the water, for many were too weak to do more than struggle feebly. Water had soaked their heaving clothing and weighted them down.

A cry rang out behind him . . . somebody was down. He drew up, giving his horse a chance to breathe. A woman had lost hold of her valise and her cry was one of anguish. No doubt the valise contained those keepsakes that a woman holds of most value, and she let go her hold on the rope and grasped frantically for it.

Instantly the swirling waters swept her from her feet. She struggled, came partly erect once more, then was knocked down by a piece of wreckage.

A tall, fine-looking man, roughly dressed and unshaved, broke from his shelter near the side of a house and caught her sleeve, helping her up. Looking past her, he saw the valise had brought up against a step, and he struggled across the street, almost breast high in the center, retrieved the valise, and brought it back. With one arm around the white-haired woman, he helped her on toward the courthouse, holding the handle of the valise in the other hand.

"That's Bill Taylor," somebody said. "Crain must have let them out of jail."

Duvarney headed his horse for the courthouse steps. Turning in the saddle, he glanced at the Munson riders. Two of them he knew, the two on the wharf at Indianola on that first day. They were looking at him, and the grin on their faces was not pleasant.

"Go ahead, Majuh," one of them said. "You get free of what you're doin'. We can wait."

Four of them . . . and there was just Welt Spicer and himself.

It was to be a fight this time, storm or no storm. Duvarney watched them sitting there in their saddles, water washing their stirrups, making no effort to help. Taylor had been a feudist, too, imprisoned for the killing of Sutton and Slaughter on a steamboat alongside the dock in Indianola; but Taylor was a gentleman and a Texan. The Munson crowd were a rabble; few of them now were even of the family, most were just a gang gathered together, fighting for whatever they could win.

"Better get inside," Duvarney said to a man who stopped at his stirrup to thank him. "I've got to go back after Brunswick and that girl."

"She gave up her place," the man said. "She stepped aside."

"She would," Duvarney said; "she's got the backbone to do it." And to follow him here, to leave a comfortable and beautiful home . . . she had come here to this and, knowing her, he knew that she would have no regrets.

He turned his horse as Welt closed in beside him. "Well, here it is, Major. We've got our fight, whether we want it or not."

"If they killed Lon Porter," Tap said, "I want it."

He swung his horse and rode toward them. Out of the corner of his eye he could see Jessica standing with Brunswick on the end of the boardwalk. He wanted to go to them, but if he did he would expose himself to the fire from the Munsons . . . and he knew they would wait no longer.

He rode right at them, his horse buck-jumping through the water. Welt had kept a little behind and on the right, working toward their flank, and they didn't like it.

"Which of you killed Lon Porter?" Tap spoke mildly.

"That gent over back of the corral who was huntin'

you?" one of them asked. It was one of the men from
the wharf who spoke. "I missed out on that. Didn't
git there soon enough. Know what he was fixin' to tell
you? We hit ol' Tom Kitt'ry t'other day an' knocked him
for a loop . . . scattered his cows, shot up all those
folks he had with him. Ol' Tom's either dead or hidin'
in a swamp somewheres. Maybe he's drowned by now."

"We come after you," the other one said. "We heard
tell ol' Jackson had staked you out for hisself, but that
ain't fair. We figured to owe you somethin' for that
mix-up down to the dock."

"Now, look, boys." Tap's voice was still mild.

He went for his gun.

Both Munsons had been holding guns under their
slickers, drawn and ready, but they were talkers, and
they wanted to tell him what they had done, and what
they planned to do.

Duvarney's gun came up fast, the hammer coming
back as the gun barrel swung up; then the hammer
dropped and he was thumbing it in a steady roll of
sound. The tallest Munson grabbed his stomach, swinging his pistol to bring it to bear, but the gun would not
fire. Evidently Tap's bullet had hit the hammer or the
trigger of the gun as Munson held it across his stomach
under the slicker, and the gun was jammed.

The bullet had glanced upward, inflicting a wound
. . . Tap could see the blood, bright crimson before the
rain hit it, even as he fired his second and third shots.

His second shot caught Munson in the chest; the
third was directed at the second Munson. He heard
guns hammering, knew Spicer and the others were
fighting. He saw the tallest Munson drop, heard the
whiff of a bullet by his face, and saw the second weav-
ing in his saddle. Even as he shot, he saw that these
men were not fighters, they were killers, an altogether
different thing. It is one thing to shoot a man from
ambush, or when outnumbering the enemy; it is quite
another thing to stand up face to face with a man who
also holds a gun, and will shoot.

Tap turned toward Spicer, but Welt had been smarter than he, for Welt had stayed off some thirty yards and used his Winchester. In the driving rain, at thirty yards he was not a good target for hasty six-gun shooting. He had shot his first man, cold-turkey, and had his Winchester .44-40 on the other when the man threw down his gun and lifted his hands.

"You all right, Welt?" Tap asked.

"Sure. You?"

"Hold that man, Welt. I want to talk to him." He walked his horse slowly through the water, keeping to the side where it was not more than stirrup-deep, and rode to where Jessica stood. Her face was very pale, her eyes unnaturally large.

"You came to a rough country, Jessica," he said.

She looked up at him, holding up her skirt in one hand, "My man was here," she said simply.

12

He bent over, offering his hand, and, gathering her skirt a little more, she stepped a toe into his stirrup, and he seated her before him.

"Tappan . . . those men . . . the ones you shot? Did you kill them?"

"They fell into four feet of water, Jessica, and I am not wasting time looking for them. When I got off the ship, two of them were on the dock and picked a fight with me simply because I was a well-dressed stranger. Now they've brought me into a feud I wanted no part of. What happened to them ceases to be my concern."

They had reached the steps of the courthouse, and he let her down gently, water swirling only inches from the step. "Better stay inside," he said. "I think we haven't seen the worst of it."

"Where are you going?"

He smiled at her. "First, I'm going to get Brunswick over here. Then Welt Spicer and me will ride back to our cattle. Will you be all right?"

"Of course, Tappan. Don't worry your head about me."

He bent over and kissed her lightly. "I'll be back," he said.

Welt Spicer took the lead. The rain had eased a little, and there seemed to be a lessening of the wind. Duvarney was sure what they had seen was only an outer edge of the storm, and the worst was yet to come. This was not the eye of the storm, but one of those curious gaps in the wind, an island of calm in the midst of fury . . . or relative calm, for rain still fell, and the wind still blew. He also knew there was little time to do what must be done.

There was no better place to stay than the courthouse. It was a strongly built structure on higher ground, and so was above the rising water, and it seemed able to withstand the wind.

Welt dropped back beside him. "Major, you'd better start considering Jackson Huddy. You'll have him to contend with."

"I know."

He had been thinking a lot about Huddy, and knew what he must do, if he could. He must find Huddy and force him into a fight. If given time, the man would surely plan an ambush and kill him in his own time, on his chosen ground. The only way to fight such a man was in the way he did not want to be fought—in the open and man to man. To do that, he must stay on Huddy's trail, find him, and either push the fight, or stay with him until Huddy had no choice.

It was easy enough to consider such a plan, but it was something else to bring it to a conclusion. It was like serving a bear steak. First you had to catch a bear.

"Hey!" Welt exclaimed. "Look over there!"

On a low ridge off to their left was a dark mass of cattle and horses. At least twenty acres of the long ridge and its flanks were above water, and they could see several riders around a fire.

Duvarney turned his mount toward them. "If they're friendly, maybe we can get some fresh horses."

They could see that there were three men and a spindling boy of fourteen or so. One of the men stood up, waiting for them.

"Hell of a storm," Duvarney said, "and there's more on the way."

"You think so? We'd about come to the notion it was over."

"Don't you believe it. Hold your stock right here. You'll see all hell break loose within the next few hours. Worse than it has been."

"Light and set," the man suggested. "You boys look played out."

They swung down and edged up to the fire, where a cowhand with a square, tough face gestured at the pot. "Help yourself," he said. "It's hot and black."

It was, hotter and blacker than the sins of the devil himself. But it tasted right.

Duvarney glanced over at the man who had spoken first, the oldest of the lot. "You want to sell some horses? Or swap? We're going to need some horses that can stand the gaff."

"You runnin' from something?" The old man eyed them sternly.

"Runnin' *at* it," Spicer said. "There's been some shootin,' and there's like to be more."

"You ain't Taylors?"

"No, but we saw Bill Taylor in town. They freed him from jail, and he risked his neck helpin' women-folks to the courthouse." Spicer looked at them over the brim of his cup. "I'm thinkin' you've seen the last of Indianola."

They stared at him. "Half of it's floatin' in the street now," Spicer went on.

The boy was interested. "You said there'd been shootin'?"

"This here's Major Tappan Duvarney," Spicer said; "he's partnered with Tom Kittery. We were taking no part in the feud, but they murdered one of our boys, and when we were helping womenfolks to get to the courthouse they came up on us. Four of 'em."

"Four?" The short puncher looked doubtful.

"The Major here, he taken two of the Munsons, shot 'em right out of the saddle. I taken one of them with my Winchester, and the other was of no mind to fight."

Welt turned suddenly. "Major, we done forgot all about him. He must've slipped off!" Spicer swore. "Major, that was my fault. I was s'posed to watch him."

"Forget it. I don't know what we'd have done with him anyhow."

"You can have the horses," the stockman said. "You want two?"

"Six," Tap said, "if you can spare them."

Over coffee and corn pone with sow belly they worked out a deal. Welt Spicer roamed restlessly, his eyes on the country around. Much of it was above water, but was a sea of mud. Water swirled in all the low places, dark brown under the somber sky.

When the bargain had been made, and Tap had paid the money, the rancher filled his cup again. "Major," he said, "ain't you the man who is driving north with a trail herd?"

Duvarney explained about the herd he had sold, and where it was, then added that Kittery's cattle had been scattered by the Munsons . . . or so he had heard.

"My name is Webster, Major, and I'm holding about two hundred head here, and I've got about thirty head of saddle stock. How about me throwing in with you for that drive?"

Tap considered. Undoubtedly, if the Munsons had told the truth, his herd was scattered, yet some might still be together, and despite the conditions he was in no mood to quit. The check he had in his pocket represented a part of his investment, but only a part. If he could round up some of the cattle—and those alive would surely be bunched on high ground and easy to find—he could start a drive anyway.

"Fine!" he said. "I'll tell you what, Webster. When the water is down enough to move, you start for Victoria. Camp on the first big bend of the Guadalupe above the town, or as near there as practical, and we'll join you there. I've an idea I'll be driving Brunswick's cattle too."

The day was nearly gone when they moved out again, holding to high ground and scouting for cattle. Here and there they found a few Rafter K steers, and several bearing Duvarney's own brand. Moving them on, he was driving about thirty head of steers when he drew rein about a mile from camp. Against the dark clouds he could see a thread of pale smoke mounting . . . the camp was there.

Welt rode up beside him and began to build a smoke. The hills were dark with evening, the low-hanging clouds turning all the shadowed hills and hollows into black and gray. The cattle were concealed in the brush and so could not be seen; the brush itself was all a uniform blackness.

"You know, Welt, take a man like Jackson Huddy, now. He'd be apt to scout around hunting us out. He could find that herd now, couldn't he?"

"I reckon so."

"And being the kind of man he is, what would he be likely to do? Figuring you were him, with his make-up, what would you do?"

Welt Spicer's cigarette glowed in the dark. After a moment, he answered. "Why, I'd locate the cattle and leave them be. In this sort of weather, they ain't goin' no place I couldn't find 'em. So I'd move out somewhere and hole up and wait for you. After all, you're one of the men I'd want to kill."

"That's what I was thinking," Duvarney said. He studied the terrain ahead of them. "Being that kind of man, where would you lie up to wait?"

In the light that remained, they studied the layout

of the country around. The low ground between the ridges and knolls was flooded, the small lakes like sheets of polished steel in the gray light. Trees and brush merged together into the darkness of the land.

The camp could be anywhere out there—not in the flooded lowlands, but on the slopes. Suddenly he made up his mind.

"We aren't going in, Welt. We'll bed down and wait right here."

"It ain't far," Welt said. "I had my mind set on hot coffee and a meal."

"I picked up some grub from Webster back there," Tap said. "We'll stay here. My theory is, never walk into an opponent when he's set. It's better to circle around and get him out of position. In this case he can come to us if he wants to."

The place they found was ideal. It was on an open slope under a brow of sand. Sixty feet out from the bank they built their fire. The sand ridge had been scoured by wind until the overhang seemed ready to collapse at any moment, but the site they chose was just beyond the limits of where the sand would come if it did fall. Certainly nobody could approach the edge of that bluff without sending the sand, and himself, tumbling down the bank, and that insured them of safety from behind.

Before them the slope fell away, covered with sparse grass for the hungry horses and cattle. Most of the night they would be moving about on the slope between the fire and any approach from below, effectively blocking any attack from that side.

The fire they built was small, and was partly shielded by a mound of wet sand they built up for the purpose. There they made coffee and fried bacon. They had little enough, but they were hungry, and when they had eaten the bacon they wiped up the grease with chunks of bread that Webster had given them.

"You sleep, Spicer," Duvarney advised. "I'll call you after a bit."

Welt hesitated. Tap had seen that Spicer was half

dead from fatigue, so he blocked any protest by adding, "I'm not tired yet, Spicer, and I've got to do some thinking. You get some sleep."

When Spicer was asleep, Tap added a few sticks to the fire and moved back from it to a spot partly sheltered by a hummock of sand and brush. The truth of the matter was he was half dead from weariness himself, but he did have thinking to do.

His plans had been shot to pieces by feud and storm. If he hoped to save anything from the wreckage, he must have another plan. Brunswick could no longer make a shipping from Indianola, and the chances were that all the Gulf ports had suffered. The thing to do, he knew, was to make a drive to Kansas, as originally planned.

The only way he could do that, even with Brunswick's help, was to strike south quickly, round up all the cattle he could find that wore his brand or that of Kittery, and then start north at once. This country would be weeks if not months recovering from the disaster, and if he moved swiftly he might even get away before any more serious fighting developed.

But, whether he liked it or not, he had to get Jackson Huddy before the killer got him. For one thing was certain: Huddy would try. Duvarney was no longer an outsider, for now he had killed Munsons.

He carefully considered every move, and then when the skies were thickening again, he shook Spicer awake.

"Can you spell me? I've about had it," he said.

Welt Spicer rolled out and slipped on his slicker. He took his rifle and slung it, muzzle down, from his shoulder. Duvarney rolled into a half-wet blanket under a tarp, and was almost instantly asleep.

Awakening suddenly, feeling the tap-tap of rain-fingers on the tarp, he lifted the edge ever so little, inhaling deeply of the fresh, rain-cooled air, and listening. He could hear the hiss and crackle of the small fire, but unless he moved he could see only the light cast by the flames, not the fire itself. He felt a curious reluctance to move, as if some subconscious warning had come to him in his sleep, awakening him.

He slid his pistol from its holster under the tarp and hooked his thumb over the hammer, easing the gun up, chest-high and ready for firing.

His ears captured no sound, his eyes could see nothing but the firelight. The wind, which had almost died away, suddenly guttered the fire, and rustled among the leaves of the brush. Ever so slightly, he tilted back his head and opened the tarp a little more. A cold drop of rain fell from the edge to his arm and trickled from his wrist toward his elbow.

Welt Spicer was seated at the fire, just far enough back to be out of its light, and his head was hanging down. Even as Duvarney saw him, Spicer's head came up. He shook it, trying to clear it of sleep, and stared all around him, holding his eyes unnaturally wide as a man does in trying to ward off sleep. He eased his position, and soon his head lowered again.

At that moment, and for no apparent reason, Duvarney glanced up toward the rim of sand that hung above their camp. His bed was made so that his feet pointed toward the bluff, and now, as he looked, he saw something round and white rising above the rim. A gleam of light appeared and vanished . . . a rifle barrel?

The spot of white lifted, and now he could make it out better. There was just enough light from the fire to reflect from the face of the man who was some yards off on the rim of sand.

For a man was there, rising up to his knees to aim his rifle into the camp. But his position was not quite what he wanted, and he hitched one knee forward. The movement was his undoing.

He was already on the very lip of the sand, and the move put his knee down on the overhang. Instantly the sand gave way and the man came tumbling down, accompanied by a great mass of sand. He hit bottom floundering, and as he struggled to his feet. Duvarney lifted himself on one elbow and shot him.

The fall of sand made only a heavy *whush* in the night, but the shot startled the animals to their feet and brought Welt Spicer up standing.

"Watch yourself, Welt. There may be more of them."

Where Welt had stood, there was emptiness, then his quiet voice came. "Sorry, Major, I must have fallen asleep."

"You were dozing. It's all right, I was awake."

"Who was it?"

Duvarney pointed. "He was drawing a bead on you from the rim, but he changed position a mite, and it toppled with him. I took his action as unfriendly, so I put the brand on him."

Duvarney remained where he was, but after a moment he ejected the empty shell from his gun and reloaded.

"I figure this man was scouting and saw his chance. Now, they heard that shot but they don't know whose it was—he might have shot one of us, or we might have shot him."

"They'll think he got one of us," Welt said. "They might not even know there was two of us here." Welt was close by now, only a few feet from Duvarney. "They'll be expectin' him back, you know."

Tap considered that. It would give a man a chance to walk right up on their camp. He could work near to it in the darkness, then just stand up and walk in. If he came right up to their fire they would be sure it was their own man, returning from whatever he had set out to do.

"I'm going down there," Tap said, "and see if Huddy is around."

"You want comp'ny?"

"They'll be expecting one man. You sit tight, . . . and take care."

Duvarney took his rifle and went down the slope. When he found their fire he saw that there were five men seated by it, or lying around, talking. They seemed unworried about the possibilities of attack, which meant they had hit Tom Kittery hard.

He went on down, making no pretence of being quiet. At the edge of the fire he saw seven saddled horses.

They looked up as he came near, and one man started to speak; then he saw Duvarney. "Sit tight, boys," Duvarney said. "I don't want to kill anybody unless I have to."

One of them was the man who had escaped from them in Indianola. "Do what he says," this man said. "This is Duvarney . . . the one I was tellin' you about."

Suddenly Tap's mind registered the significant fact that there were five men here. He had killed one up at his camp, and yet there were seven saddled horses . . . *where was the other man?*

"Where's Jackson Huddy?" he asked.

One of the men grinned. "Don't try to find him. He'll find you."

"I hear he's something of a man hunter," Tap responded, "but as near as I can find out he never met anybody in a fair, stand-up shooting match. Anybody can run up a score hiding out in the brush."

It was a deliberate taunt. He wanted Jackson Huddy to hear it. He wanted to anger him, to jar him out of his usual pattern. He wanted that slow, meticulous, careful man to be jolted into acting quickly.

"Man, you're askin' for trouble!"

"I shouldn't really ask, I expect," Duvarney said carelessly. "From all I hear, he's so used to crawling on his belly in the grass that he wouldn't know how to stand up and fight."

"Jackson Huddy never went after a man yet that he didn't get," one of the men said. "You'll be the next, mister."

"Well, you just tell him I was around. And don't forget the name. I wouldn't want him to miss seeing me. . . . And you tell him that if he doesn't want to meet me face to face I'll do a little stalking myself."

He backed off into the darkness, still holding the rifle easy in his hands.

Returning to his own fire, he told Spicer briefly what he had done, and doused water over the coals.

"I want to get him out of the brush if I can, but I'm not going to wait. I'm going after him . . . now. He'll be over there somewhere near our camp, but let's scatter those other boys, anyway."

They rounded up the small bunch of cattle they had. He let out a whoop and fired his pistol. It needed only that to start them running, and he headed them toward his other camp, right across the slope where the Munson fire was.

They heard the cattle coming, and in the dim light Duvarney saw them scattering, horses and men. Only one shot was fired, and then the cattle went storming through the camp, churning the fire into the ground, and men and horses fled.

One man had caught up his rifle, and now he tried to swing it around to bear on Duvarney, but Spicer rode down on him. Too late, the man tried to wheel to fire at Spicer, and then the charging horse hit him and knocked him rolling in the mud.

They went up the slope on the run, and Duvarney's riders came rushing out, ready for a fight.

"Mount up," he said, "and keep moving." Crouching low in his saddle, he skirted the dark brush, hunting in the gray light for tracks where a man might have gone in.

If the seventh man was Huddy, as Tap suspected, he had to be hidden somewhere in the brush where he could wait for a shot at Duvarney. It would be natural for Duvarney to return to his campfire and his men, and a man might by searching find a good spot from which to shoot at his target.

A moving target would be something of a problem, for any hiding place that Huddy might crawl into that would allow him to get in sight of the camp would be in dense brush where swinging a rifle would be difficult, and finding a clear field of fire in more than one direction would be impossible.

Twice Tap stopped on the windward side of the brush and, digging beneath the surface of the leaves, sought for some dry enough to burn. He did not hope for a real fire, wet as it was, but for a good smoke, a smoke that might drive him out.

"He's afoot, anyway," Lawton Bean commented. "The way you scattered their horses, that whole outfit is afoot."

The fire smoked and, blazing a little, ate away at the edges of the leaves, fighting against the dampness. The smoke drifted through the brush, as he had hoped it would.

Duvarney considered the situation, and liked none of it. The rain would undoubtedly put out the feeble fires he had started, probably before they had developed sufficient smoke to drive Huddy, if it was Huddy, from concealment. The smoke might cause him some discomfort, but nothing more. In the meanwhile, it might be a long wait, and Huddy might find a place where he could get a good shot at them. And all this time Tom Kittery was in trouble to the south, and that was where the cattle would be.

From the very beginning, he was thinking, nothing had gone well. He had hoped to land in Texas, find a gathered herd ready to move, and start at once for Kansas. Instead, he had found his partner involved in a killing feud to the point where all business had been neglected; and to be on the safe side Tap had had to recruit his own men. They had gathered cattle, only to be interrupted by the storm, yet he had sold cattle and had the check in his pocket.

Now, like it or not, he was involved in the feud. One of his men had been killed; he himself had been attacked, and he had killed in return. Yet he wanted nothing more than to be on the trail to Kansas.

The cattle would be, he surmised, on high ground. Bunched by the storm, they would be ready for a drive.

He was torn between the need to find Kittery, to round up a herd, and to locate Huddy and force him into a showdown.

He made up his mind. He would have to chance Huddy. First things must come first; and he must find Tom Kittery, and get a herd on the trail to Kansas.

But even as he turned away, he was haunted by fear. Jackson Huddy was no man to be trifled with, and Jackson Huddy would be hunting him like a wolf trailing for a kill.

From now on, no moment, waking or sleeping, would be without fear.

13

Bunching the cattle, they started them westward. Driving them down off the ridge, they waded them and swam them until they had put a good mile behind them. Then they found the ground above water, but soggy and miserable.

The cattle moved sullenly. The rain had ceased, but the sky remained dark and heavily overcast, and they could hear thunder in the distance. The wind was rising.

During the incessant blowing of the past two days the wind had become almost a part of their lives, and the time before that was wiped out, almost as if it had never been. To Tap Duvarney it seemed as if he could not remember a time when he had not been wet and cold, and harried by wind.

Leaving Belden in charge, he took Spicer and Lawton Bean and they headed south.

"In this weather," Bean said, "we ain't got a chance of findin' them. They'll be holed up somewhere, if they're alive." Every word had to be shouted to be heard above the rising wind.

"We've got to try," Tap yelled, and they kept on.

The earth was black beneath, the sheets of water like steel under the heavy sky, and the dark slim trunks of the few trees were like prison bars.

At noon they came to a cabin where there was a corral, and a lean-to stable half hidden in the brush. A thin line of smoke was rising from the cabin, and with rifles ready, they hailed the door.

It opened a slit, and a thin, mustached face peered out, saw the rifles, and started to close the door, but Duvarney rode forward. "Hold it, there! We're ridin' the grub line—how about some coffee?"

The door opened wider. "All right, put your horses up and come on in, but come peaceful. I'm holdin' a Colt revolvin' shotgun."

The cabin was snug, overly warm, and dry. The squatter had not lied . . . he had the shotgun right at hand, and he was wearing a six-shooter.

"Never turned away a hungry man yet," he said, "but you boys rode up holdin' a lot of shootin' power."

"We're hunting some friends," Duvarney told him. "Hear anything of a fight down this way?"

"I heard it . . . seen some of it. That was eight, maybe nine mile southeast of here. I'd been down to Refugio after grub . . . had a couple of pack mules. I was nigh to Horseshoe Lake when somebody busted loose with a war right close by. I pulled off into the brush and kept quiet. It was quite a scrap, by the sound of it."

He was a talkative man, as men who live alone are inclined to be when company shows up. He moved about, dishing up beans from a big crock, getting out some homemade bread, and putting on the frying pan. "You boys just set still an' don't go to pullin' leather. I'll roust you up some grub."

He squinted at them with inquisitive blue eyes. "You boys don't have the Munson look. Must be kin of the Kitt'ry's."

"I am Tappan Duvarney, Tom Kittery's partner."

"Figured you was kin or somethin'. Well, you won't find much left . . . cattle scattered hell to breakfast . . . Roy Kitt'ry's dead . . . Joe Breck is dead."

"How about Tom? How about Lubec and the Cajun?"

"Hid out, more'n likely. Looks like them sorry Munsons got the upper hand. Ain't been a Munson killed in quite a spell."

As they ate the old man told them of several small herds of Rafter K cattle and where they could be found.

"How are you fixed for horses?" Duvarney asked. "We could use some."

"Fix you up, all right." He gestured toward the corral. "Go have a look."

Duvarney got up slowly, surreptitiously watching his host, who was busy over the fire . . . too busy. Tap stretched, yawned, and glanced out the window at the corral. It was close to the brush on one side, where some post oak provided shade for the stock. He could see several horses in the corral, and he glanced around at Spicer.

Welt was smiling, and he had a Colt in his hand. "You go have that look, Major, and if I hear a shot, I'll kill the cook."

The old man stiffened up, turning, half ready to reach for his shotgun, but Lawton Bean had it, and he was smiling, too. "How about it, old man? You still want the Major to look at your horses? It's all right with us—on'y at the first shot we're goin' to cut you in two."

"What else could I do?" the old man said. "If I warned you, they'd shoot me. An' that there Huddy, he'd come after me. And like I said, you boys are losin' the fight."

"Don't be too sure," Bean drawled. "The Major here, he taken two Munsons just yesterday. He killed Eggen an' Wheeler Munson. Welt Spicer here, he nailed another one of that outfit. And last night one of 'em tried to dry-gulch us an' he cashed in his chips mighty fast."

The old man looked from one to the other. "I ain't no coward, and I don't like Munsons, but what can I I do? I'm alone out here, an' with that Huddy around . . ."

"He won't be around long," Spicer said.

"What's out there?" Duvarney asked quietly.

"Three of 'em. They stopped by to get out of the storm but when they saw you comin' they headed for the brush, figurin' to lay out an' pick you off, easy like."

Duvarney stood well back inside, but he was looking out the window, studying the environment with care.

"One of them is Pinto Hart," the old man offered, "an' he ain't no schoolboy."

"They call him Pinto because of a scar on his face," Spicer said. "He's a brother to Jim Hart, and they're two of the top men in the Munson crowd."

Tap went from window to window, looking at the surroundings. When he had found what he was looking for, he turned back to the room. He gestured toward the moccasins the old man wore. "Have you got another pair of those?"

"I might have."

"I'm buying them," Tap said; "get them out."

The old man opened a chest and removed several pairs of trousers, some shirts, and then the moccasins. "I traded 'em off a squaw. They're new . . . never worn."

Duvarney dropped a silver dollar on the table. "You probably didn't give her half that," he said. Then he sat down and slipped off his boots and put on the moccasins. They were a surprisingly good fit.

"You boys sit tight," he said to the others. "Keep an eye on that bunch out there, and if Dad here gives you any trouble, tie him up."

"Now what kinda talk is that?" the old man complained. "I'm no Munson, and I'm not huntin' trouble." He paused, watching Duvarney hitch his bowie knife around, ready to hand. "Did you hear me right? There's three of them out there . . . an' Pinto's worth two or three all by himself."

Tap ignored him; then, like a ghost, he slipped from the door. Outside, the wind was blowing and a light rain was falling. He went around the cabin to get it between himself and the hidden men, and dropping to a crouch, moved behind a bush, hesitated a moment, and slipped beyond to a tree.

He had fought too many Indians and stalked too much wild game not to know how it was done. The moccasins could feel of the earth beneath, avoiding any stick that might break. . . . He moved deeper into the brush. He carried no rifle, preferring to depend on his two pistols and the knife.

He scouted wide, moving with the wind to cover any sound, his eyes watchful. The trees bent under the wind, and a spattering of huge drops fell on the leaves, and on his head and shoulders.

It was a game of death he was playing, but a game he had played before. These men, so far as he knew, were cowhands, men who rode horseback. They were not woodsmen in the sense he had been. Now, if the Cajun were out there. . . . He had a feeling about the Cajun . . . *there* was a dangerous man.

There was a weird, yellowish light in the trees. This was a fairly large patch of ground, covering fifteen to twenty acres, part of it running down to a stream bed. He took his time, knowing that death awaited a careless hunter, but he moved in closer.

Suddenly he stopped. Not far ahead he could see the light beyond the trees, and knew that he must be somewhere within a hundred yards of the men he hunted—very likely much less than that.

He had paused behind a bush, with two trees in line behind him, and another one only inches to the left. No one looking in his direction would guess that a man stood there. He studied the leaves and the brush about him with care.

His eyes scanned the woods ahead of him, looking across a leaf-filled hollow where the slow drops fell from arching branches above, when he saw them. They were bunched as he had hoped they would be, and were seated where they could watch the cabin and anyone who approached the corral.

They were closer than he had thought—only about twenty-five yards away. The gun he carried in his holster was a Smith & Wesson Russian .44, the straightest-shooting gun in the West at the time. At that distance he had often scored high at target shooting. This was not so easy, for the background made it difficult, the men and their clothing merging well with the trees and brush.

He moved a step forward, putting his foot down with the utmost care, and letting it sink into the wet leaves. Then he took another step. As he moved, his mind was telling him that at that distance he would probably do better than they could, for though they were used to guns, they were not likely to have had as thorough a training as he had had, nor the experience in the cavalry.

He took a third step—each step was a short one. They would turn soon, and that was the way he wanted it. He did not want to surprise them into shooting. If possible, he would take them without any shooting, and without killing.

He stood now beneath a huge pecan tree and looked at the three men across the small hollow. They were talking quietly, and smoking. He smiled at that. An Apache would have smelled that smoke—as he had —long before he saw them.

One of the men knocked out his pipe against his heel, a sound that would carry too far . . . these men were not the sort he was used to dealing with. The man started to put his pipe in his pocket, and he turned just a little as his hand reached back for his coat pocket. With that motion his head turned slightly to the right, as it often will with such a movement, and he saw Duvarney.

He froze with the movement half completed, staring hard, obviously unwilling to believe what he saw, or unsure of it. The position in which Duvarney was standing would be even worse for them to see clearly than was their position for Tap.

"Pinto," he said. "Pinto . . . *look*."

When Pinto turned his head Tap saw the scar . . . a bad powder burn, he would guess, although it was impossible to tell at that distance.

"You boys waiting for me?" Duvarney asked in a conversational tone. "There doesn't have to be a shooting, you know. You can just shuck your guns and back off. I'm down here on business—I'm not trying to run up a score."

They looked at him, unwilling to believe that he was actually there, that he had moved up behind them without their knowing it. It offended their pride . . . after all, they were fighting men.

He held the Smith & Wesson in his hand, the muzzle down slightly, but ready.

"You'd better do that," he added. "Just loosen your gun belts and let them fall."

Pinto Hart was getting slowly to his feet—slowly and carefully. Tap watched them all without any partiality, and he could catch any move. When Pinto was on his feet, he said, "I'll be damned if I will."

"You boys better talk to him. I shoot pretty straight, but at this distance I might nail any one of you. I'll surely get him, but one of you might get hurt."

One of the two men sitting there had a rifle across his knees, but he would have to swing ninety degrees to bring it to bear . . . it would take too long, and the man knew it. The other man was the one who put the pipe in his pocket, and his hand was still there, clutching the pipe. Nobody wants to die, and this man knew he had a good chance of not living out the next two minutes, and he was sweating.

"Talk to him, boys," Tap said again, "or pull him down. He'll only get you killed."

"Pinto?" The man with the rifle was speaking. "I think—"

Pinto took a step back and went for his gun. Tap hesitated a fraction of a second to see what the others would do, and then shot Pinto Hart through the lower right corner of his breast pocket. He fired only once, then held his fire.

"How about it, boys? What's in it for you that will weigh as heavy as a bullet in the head?"

Very carefully the man with the rifle pitched it from him, and unbuckled his belt. The other man moved gingerly to do the same.

"Why don't you boys just head for Refugio and take the stage on west? Arizona's a good country. So's New Mexico."

They turned with great care and, stiff-backed, walked away as Duvarney followed them. He glanced once at the body of Pinto Hart. A tough, reckless man, and a game one. It was a pity, but he had thought of himself as a good man with a gun, and that kind of belief can get a man killed. A reputation for being tough can give a man some standing with his fellows, but there always comes a time when he has to back it up . . . and the same men who praised your skill will sneer at it by comparison with the man who shoots you.

"We got to get our horses," one of the men said.

"Walk," Duvarney said. "A good walk in the rain and the wind will give you time to consider your ways. And boys—be sure you take that stage. If I saw you around I might just think you were waiting for me, and I'd have to shoot on sight, I wouldn't want to do that."

He watched them go, and then he walked back to the cabin and went in the door.

The old man was tipped back in his chair, and he let the chair legs down hard when Duvarney came in. Welt Spicer merely gave Tap a satisfied look, and Lawton Bean stretched.

"Two of them are walking to Refugio," Duvarney said. "It will cool them off a bit."

"Pinto?" the old man asked quickly.

"Pinto's out there. Will you take care of him, *amigo?* We'll take those horses, too," he added. "I think we're going to need them, the way the weather is."

"You killed Pinto Hart?" The old man could not find it in himself to believe it could happen that way.

"He killed himself," Duvarney said. "He made an error in judgment."

They rode to the south and then east, and within a few miles they began to see Rafter K cattle.

14

Jessica Trescott huddled in her mackintosh, half asleep. The wind filled the day with a dreadful roaring, like nothing she had ever heard. Outwardly, Jessica was calm; inwardly, she trembled. It was a trembling down deep inside her, the trembling of a fear such as she had never known.

The others were gathered about her, together yet alone; for in a terrible storm each person is alone within their minds, cowering with their own private fears, their uncertainties. There is no isolation like that brought on by storm, for the voice cannot rise above the wind, nor can it reach that private place within the head where man hovers in the midst of all that he is and has been.

Jessica's hands were thrust deep in her pockets, her shoulders were hunched, as much to shut out the sound as to bring warmth.

The courthouse was of concrete, and it was strongly built. The rise of ground on which it sat lifted it somewhat above the waters.

142

And now, for the first time, the great waves began to break over the island.

Up to now the wind had driven the waters of the bay upon the shore, had driven great volumes of water through the passages between the islands, and the swells had pounded the outer islands, but only now had the sea begun to roll its swells clear across the island and up on the low shores.

It began in the town with a mighty wave that sent a rolling wall of water up the street. This was almost immediately followed by another. The outer buildings of the town, battered by the gigantic winds, now crashed before the onrushing sea.

"Ma'am?"

Jessica looked up to see Bill Taylor standing beside her, hat in hand. "Ma'am," he repeated, "you got to see this. Maybe you'll never see the like again."

With Mady and Bob Brunswick, she followed him up the stairs to the second floor. Up there she was conscious only of the mighty sound of the wind. The building seemed to give before the weight of it pressing against the walls. It even seemed to suck the breath from her lungs, causing her to gasp for each breath. When he led her to a window with a broken shutter, she looked out over Indianola and was appalled.

As far as her eyes could see, in the intervals between the gusts of wind and rain, there was only water. The rushing waves were smashing the buildings now, floating the less securely anchored, sending them crashing one against another with tremendous, splintering force.

There was no longer a harbor, no longer any piers to be seen, or any land at all. Here and there a tree, rooted more deeply than the others, still held its place, almost drowned by the rising water.

The boardwalk where she had stood not long ago was gone, and the hotel itself canted over weirdly. For a moment she thought of her clothing there . . . of the pictures of her father and mother, her diary . . . all would be gone, carried away by the flood.

Mady was thinking of those dresses, too. "All those beautiful gowns!" she wailed.

Jessica glanced at her, and said wryly, "I don't believe those clothes have much to do with what is really worth-while, and I doubt if Tappan will even realize they are gone."

"I wish I had them."

"The only things I regret are a few personal keep-sakes and my books, and I haven't really lost them, I suppose. Once you have read a book you care about, some part of it is always with you."

She looked out at the frightful havoc of the storm. A town was dying out there, being wiped from the earth, but guiltily she realized that all she could think about was Tappan. Where was he? Was he safe?

The worst of it was, there was nothing she could do. Those who could reach the courthouse were there. Bill Taylor and a few others had performed amazingly, res-cuing men, women, and children, and getting them all inside. Taylor, awaiting trial for his part in a shooting, had worked harder than anyone in getting people to safety.

She went back and sat down. The water was over the steps now, and the town was simply caving in under the combined attack of sea and wind.

Here and there clusters of men bunched together. Once Taylor came over and squatted near by. He knew Mady, of course, but it was to Jessica he talked. "Stories are going around," he said, "that there's been more shooting south of here. But don't you worry; that man of yours is a good hand. I watched him out there against Eggen and Wheeler. He'll take care of himself."

He did not look at Mady or speak to her. Once she started to address him and he pointedly looked away. She flushed.

"Tom Kitt'ry," Taylor said, "ran into a bunch of trouble. Seems they knew right where to find him, and they did. Feller rode into town . . . he's downstairs right now . . . he heard Pete Remley and Joe Breck were dead . . . Roy Kitt'ry too. Tom's hurt, an' he's hid out. Somebody wished him no good," Taylor added insinuatingly, "and folks know it. If there ever was a talker, it was that show-off, Ev Munson."

From the corners of her eyes, Jessica looked at Mady. Her face was shockingly white and pinched. She seemed shrunken, somehow, and she stared straight ahead in a kind of stark shame.

"Tom's goin' to win now. That man of yours, Duvarney—he makes the dif'rence. Those men he's got, they're good ones, but it's Duvarney . . . he's outguessed them every turn."

After a while, Taylor moved away, and the two girls sat silent. Finally, Jessica could restrain herself no longer. "Mady . . . why did you do it?"

"Oh . . . *you!* You think you know so much! How do you know how it is to live in a place like this, year after year? I wanted Tom to leave. I wanted him to get out. And I knew he never would as long as that crazy feud was going on! Anyway, I had nothing to do with what happened."

"I saw you talking to Every Munson, Mady."

"What if you did? I've known Ev Munson all my life. I never cared about their silly feud. All I wanted was for Tom to take me away."

"Away from all he knew? Did that seem wise, Mady? This is Tom's life. He knows cattle. He knows the range, the people. In the city he would be just another man struggling for a living among men who had grown up in a life he had never known."

"Tom would do all right," Mady said defiantly.

"And so you betrayed him?"

Mady turned on Jessica, her eyes hot with anger. "I did no such thing!"

"I think you did, Mady. I also think you were there when Lon Porter was killed."

Mady was silent. After a moment she said, "I did see that, but I had nothing to do with it. When I got to the corral Lon Porter was tying up his horse and asking for

Major Duvarney. He said he had a message from Tom.
. . . Well, he talked too loud and Jackson Huddy heard
him."

"Did Jackson Huddy kill him?"

"Yes, he did. He shot him through the back of the
head, and I saw it. Oh, he didn't see me, and I was
so scared I couldn't move if I'd wanted to! Jackson
Huddy wasn't more than thirty feet from him, and Lon
Porter never knew anybody else was around, and you
can just bet that hostler isn't going to tell of it."

The wind was rising, and talk was becoming impossible. Sheets of rain battered the walls, seeping through
around window casings and falling in huge drops from
the ceilings. Outside, almost nothing could be seen, and
nobody wanted to risk standing near enough to a window even to try.

All of those on the ground floor had now climbed
the stairs, for water was coming through under the
doors, and one of the windows had been smashed by
the wind. The wild banshee howling of the storm was
maddening, and Jessica crouched on a bench, her legs
drawn up under her, her head sunk behind the collar of
her mackintosh, and her hands over her ears.

Once, Taylor caught her shoulder and pointed. A
window had smashed and water was pouring in, blown
by the howling wind. A momentary lull gave them a
glimpse of the town . . . only there was no town, only
a torn and ravaged sea, littered with wreckage and the
hull of a bottom-up ship. Then the streaming rain and
blown spray shut out the sight again.

Cowering on her bench, Jessica could only clutch herself and wait.

Tappan Duvarney and his men were scattered widely
when the wind came. Duvarney himself had found
some thirty head of cattle on a slope and started moving
them inland. Soon he had come upon a dozen more,
all steers in this lot, bedded down on a long ridge.

He had driven them no more than a mile when Lawton Bean appeared, driving thirty-odd head of mixed stuff. Some distance off they could see a long ridge running roughly north and south, and they started for it, picking up a few head from the country between.

Welt Spicer came up driving a small herd, and they bunched them on the ridge, somewhat in the lee of the rocky crest that was tufted with stunted trees and low brush. There, under a deep hollowed-out space in the rock, they found where men had occasionally taken shelter. A crude wall of piled-up stone had been built to offer even more shelter, and when the wind came they brought their horses under the overhang.

Thunder was now an almost continuous sound, and lightning flared again and again, lighting up the deep shadows under the overhang. The darkness was like late twilight. The rain roared down, slashing at the skin like cutting knives whenever one got within its range.

Spicer sat in the farthest corner of the cavelike space and stared out at the storm. All the men, for fear of lightning, had placed their guns some distance away from them. Suddenly Bean looked around at Tap. "I thought I heard a yell!" he shouted. *"Listen!"*

Duvarney went close to the mouth of the cave and waited, but for several minutes he heard nothing; then faint and far off, he heard what sounded like a shout.

"Somebody is out there needing help," he said. "You sit tight, and I'll have a look."

"Don't be loco," Spicer objected. "A feller often hears such sounds in a storm."

Drawing the string under his chin a little tighter, and turning up his collar again, Duvarney hesitated only briefly, then plunged into the wall of water outside. His heels skidded on the muddy surface, and he almost fell, then he turned and started to clamber up the slope toward the crest of the ridge, clinging to the brush to help him climb.

He could see that on the top of the ridge the trees were bent at an impossible angle, their roots still holding but the trunks almost parallel with the ground beneath. He clung to some brush, half crouching, and looked at the top of the ridge.

No man could stand erect there. The wind would blow him right off. He turned and looked all around. He could see nothing but the driving rain. Below the ridge all was a swirling mass of water from the swollen creeks. The cattle were huddled just under the crest of the long ridge, taking what shelter they could from the onslaught of the storm.

A feeble shout made him turn his head again, and he saw them. Past the point of the ridge where the slope fell away to the creek bottom a man was struggling with a mired horse, a horse that carried a dark, humped bundle on its back.

Duvarney fought his way along the ridge through the brush. One look and he could see that the man was staggering with weariness. Once he fell to his knees and could barely struggle up. Duvarney yelled and ran to him, stumbling and falling himself, skidding on his knees. He got up, reaching the man just as he was about to fall into the water.

It was Tom Kittery.

Tap led him back to the slope, where he made him sit down, and then he caught up the reins on the horse. "Come on, boy!" he called. "Let's get you out of here!"

The horse needed little help, only a little more than Tom Kittery was able to give in his exhausted condition. He struggled, forefeet clambering at the bank, but with Duvarney's help he struggled free. It was only then that Duvarney looked to see who was on his back. Two men . . . or bodies . . . wrapped in their slickers so as to shelter their heads, and tied to the horse's back.

Grabbing Tom by the arm, Duvarney pulled him erect. Just then he saw Lawton Bean and Spicer coming toward him in a tumbling run.

"Wondered what was keepin' you!" Spicer yelled.

With Bean supporting Kittery, and Spicer walking alongside, they got back to the shelter of the overhang.

Once they were out of the immediate roar and rush of the storm, it was like a reprieve from some ghastly hell, or from a wind-tortured world where one gasped for every breath, struggled to make every step.

Duvarney untied the men on the horse, and saw that they were the Cajun and Lubec. Both were wounded. The Cajun was stretched out on his slicker, and Lubec helped himself to a corner and leaned back, breathing hoarsely. One of Lubec's arms was clumsily bandaged and in a crude splint.

"What happened to that?" Spicer asked.

"Horse fell on me," Lubec grumbled. "Slipped on a bank." He indicated the Cajun. "That one's been shot. Caught two slugs."

A long time later, with the wounded men cared for and Tom in an exhausted sleep, Tap Duvarney slept, too.

Outside the storm still raged, thunder crashed and reverberated against the hills, but he slept.

15

When the morning came, the storm was gone. A few scattered clouds, ragged with a memory of yesterday's winds, still remained in the sky. Only a small wind blew, and there was no rain.

Tappan Duvarney stood at the opening of the overhang and looked out across the rain-soaked landscape. Everywhere were evidences of the hurricane's passing. Trees were down, streams still rushed bank-full, and great pools of water were everywhere over the land.

He went outside and looked along the ridge. The cattle were up, beginning to move around, seeking out the sparse grass. Half a mile away he could see another slope, also dark with cattle.

Welt Spicer came out, hitching his gun belt into place. "What's up, Major?"

"We're going to move cattle," Duvarney said grimly. "When we get some chow we're going to check out that bunch yonder. If there's any Rafter K stuff there, we'll drift it north along with what we have."

"What about them?" Spicer motioned behind them.

"The Cajun's got to have treatment. If we can find that buckboard—"

"I know where it is. Come across it t'other day. Do you want I should ride up there and get it?"

Duvarney checked his watch. It was not yet five o'clock in the morning. There were several hundred head of cattle on this ridge, and nearly as many on the other. He went to his saddlebags for his field glasses and climbed to the top of the ridge. From there, studying the terrain, he saw that, as he had suspected, there were cattle and occasionally horses on every rise within sight. Some of those must be from the scattered herds or ungathered cattle wearing the Rafter K brand.

Spicer had coffee boiling when he came back. The Cajun was lying on his back, half reclining against the wall.

"A man would think you'd been hurt," Tap said, grinning. "You mean it only took two slugs to put you down?"

"Maybe I'm gettin' weak in my old age." The Cajun's eyes searched his. "You find many cow, yes?"

"Plenty. Can you sit it out here while we round them up? Then we'll get the buckboard and you can ride in that when we drive them."

"I be all right. You go along."

Tom Kittery was on his feet. "I'm ready to ride if you are, Tap," he said quietly. "I'm beginning to think you're right. We should be in the cattle business."

"How about you?" Duvarney looked over at Lubec.

Johnny Lubec had changed none at all. "I'll handle as many cows as any of you, busted arm and all, but I'd rather stay and fight."

"Welt, you ride south with Johnny. Start all the Rafter K stock north and west. If you see trouble coming, come on back this way and we'll meet it together. But if you see Jackson Huddy, come running for me, fast."

They looked at him.

"I've staked him out," Tap said quietly. "When he killed Lon he killed a man of mine; and besides, he's the one who's out to stop us. When we get this drive started I'm going to cut out and go after him."

"Who's huntin' trouble now?" Lubec said.

"It's a safety precaution. If there was any other way I'd leave him until later. But I'm going to hunt the hunter."

"He'll kill you," Lubec said.

"Well," Tom said, "Huddy ain't never got me, and Tap here took me alive . . . although," he added, grinning, "I don't believe he could do it again."

Bean worked east, and Tom Kittery with Duvarney himself rode north. By noon they had brought the cattle down off the high ground, and had then waded them and swum them until they could get them to still higher ground west and north of Horseshoe Lake.

Lawton Bean was the last man to come along. None of the cattle were in a mood to cause trouble. After the fury of the storm, they seemed to welcome the presence of men and drifted ahead of them as if they realized they were driving them to safety.

It was almost sundown before Bean came in. He was riding with his rifle across his saddle.

"Picked up some sign back yonder," he said to Tap. "I think we're goin' to have comp'ny."

"How many?"

"One man . . . it's Huddy, all right, and he's ridin' his killin' horse."

When Duvarney looked his question, Bean added, "Folks down here tell me when Jackson Huddy goes huntin' he rides a blaze-face roan. Good, steady horse . . . hard one to see . . . lots of bottom, and quiet."

"That's a good horse," Kittery agreed. "I know him."

"I picked up some hairs off a tree where he'd been scratching himself." Bean looked at Duvarney. "Since the rain stopped."

"You didn't see him?"

When Bean shook his head, Kittery said, "I'll lay five to one he saw you. And that means he trailed you back here."

"Tom," Duvarney said, "I've got Belden and some of the boys holding a herd on the Guadalupe just west of Victoria. Most of them are cattle I sold to Bob Brunswick, just before the storm." He touched his shirt pocket. "I've got the check right here."

"You moved fast."

"We had to, with the storm coming, and then I moved the cattle for Brunswick. What I'm suggesting now is that you push this herd on to join those cattle."

"What about you?"

"I'm heading for Indianola. My girl's there. Also," he went on, "I want Jackson Huddy to follow me."

He had been thinking as he talked. Riding with a herd would not only make him a sitting duck, but would endanger the others. What he must do was lead Huddy down the trail, and it was a trail that Duvarney now knew pretty well himself . . . and somewhere along that trail there might be a showdown.

He already had part of his route planned. He would ride right out in plain sight, but where there was no cover for Huddy, and then when he got to where there was cover, he would ride right into it.

"You're buckin' a stacked deck," Tom said. "I think we'd best stick together."

"No, I want him to come for me."

"Don't worry," Lubec said, "he will!"

Duvarney left the herd on a bare hill with no cover for several hundred yards in either direction. He decided that he could take it for granted that Huddy was a good shot with a rifle, but he would also remember that Huddy, now at least, was not a gambler. Huddy would study his victim, stay with him until he got within easy range, then shoot him down. From all he had heard, Huddy was a one-shot killer . . . it was even a matter of pride with him.

That meant Duvarney must not give him that one shot until he was ready to do so.

He rode north, scouting the land and the possible routes that Huddy might take, and then he began a bit of mental warfare. Huddy would be looking for a pattern, and for a time he must not find one. Duvarney felt that first he must shake Huddy's overweening confidence in himself. He must worry him into acting as he had not planned.

For two miles he kept to open country that offered no concealment. Dropping behind a screening ridge, he wheeled his horse and raced back a quarter of a mile in the direction from which he had come, then rode down into a sandy wash. He followed it for half a mile and, climbing out of it, went to a thicket of mesquite, prickly pear, and oak. Doubling back, he scouted his earlier trail with care, finally emerging upon it.

Sure enough, another horse had been along here. He rode on across his trail without a stop, went over a low saddle, and headed back in the original direction, paralleling his old trail. Finding a long, shallow pool of muddy water, he rode into it and followed it along for a few hundred yards, then deliberately he cut across it.

A pursued man will usually emerge from a stream on the same side on which he entered; knowing this, he did the opposite. Mounting a low hill, he crossed over it and left his horse tied to a small shrub while he crept back to the crest of a ridge where there were a few scattered stones and some low brush. Lying there, he settled down to wait.

He had his back to the sun, and so could use his glasses without fear of being seen. He was lying there watching when he saw, far off, a rider approach the place where the trails crossed. He smiled, but he continued to watch, knowing he must understand this man and his thinking if he expected to remain alive.

Jackson Huddy seemed to be a man of little imagination—hard, dangerous, and tenacious, and above all a man of enormous ego, completely confident of his own ability. But always before Huddy had been the hunter, never the hunted. By now he realized that Duvarney had circled around, and knew he was being followed.

Jackson Huddy sat his horse for some time, then

followed the trail. When he reached the pond he rode along the edge, then circled it until he discovered where Duvarney had emerged. When Huddy finally saw where Duvarney had left the water, he was scarcely three hundred yards off, and Duvarney took up his rifle and drew a careful bead on the dirt right in front of Huddy's horse . . . and fired.

It was muddy, and when the bullet struck it splattered mud, and Huddy's horse leaped wildly, and pitched hard until Huddy got him quieted down. Then Duvarney shot twice more; both were shots calculated to start Huddy moving.

Tap knew he should kill the man, yet it went against the grain to shoot from ambush, even though that was the policy of his enemy; moreover, he took a wicked satisfaction in putting the man in the place of his victims.

Huddy, out in the open with no cover, slapped the spurs to his mount and went away from there as if somebody had set fire to his coattails.

Tap mounted up and rode at a canter, heading back toward Indianola. Huddy, shaken, would be wary about picking up the trail, and that would give Duvarney time.

As he rode, he studied the country, and an hour later he found what he wanted—a small hollow in the hills, ideal for a nooning, which could be looked into from only one direction. On the crest of a low rise there was a small clump of brush and trees.

Taking a branch of one of the trees, he bent it down in such a way that if one wanted to look down into the hollow, the branch must be moved. Then he cut a branch, took a piggin string from his belt, and bending the branch, made a small, crude bow of it. He sharpened a stick for an arrow and set the bow in position, the arrow drawn back and ready.

If the branch was moved, the arrow would be released and might hit the hunter.

It was a crude, hastily contrived trap that Duvarney

did not expect to cause any damage. All he hoped to do was to shake Huddy's confidence, to make him feel he could trust himself nowhere.

Going down into the hollow, Duvarney built a small fire; then back at the edge he gathered enough brush to make a large armful and tied another piggin string around it. Looked at from above, it would create a shadow, and might give the appearance of a man in hiding. At least Huddy would want to take time to study it.

Time was running short now, and Huddy might appear at any moment, so Tap rode away swiftly, but watched the hills around, careful to avoid any place that might offer Huddy a good field of fire.

Hours later he crossed Black Bayou and made camp in a clump of trees and brush northeast of Green Lake.

Before daylight he was up, and for half an hour he studied the country around. Then he left his camp and went back for half a mile in the direction from which he had come, circling wide around before riding for Indianola. He saw nobody, found no tracks leading toward Indianola.

He rode on, seeing on every side the havoc created by the storm—trees uprooted, buildings smashed flat, the earth a sea of mud, with water standing in the low places. Here and there he saw the bodies of dead cattle or horses.

When at last he rode up to Indianola he knew it only by the courthouse.

Where the town had stood there was now mud and sand, with scattered debris brought in by the sea, smashed boats, and the foundations of the buildings.

The town was gone . . . wiped out.

People were moving around, searching for bodies or prowling among the wreckage of the saloons for unbroken bottles or whatever might be found.

Smoke was rising from the chimney of the courthouse, and when he walked inside he walked right into

Bob Brunswick. "She's in there," Brunswick pointed. "We're trying to feed everybody, at least."

Duvarney explained about the cattle. "We've got a bunch together, and we're going to drive to Kansas. I figured you'd want your stock to go along. A man named Webster is throwing in with us, and we'll have a strong party and about fifteen hundred head, or more."

"Take them along. You going to Dodge?"

"Yes. I'll meet you there, or leave word if we've gone elsewhere. It doesn't look as if you'll be buying stock in Indianola for a long time."

Suddenly Jessica appeared in the door. She ran to him caught him by the arms. "Tappan! Oh, Tappan!" was all that she could say.

"We're leaving," he said. "We're getting out of here right now. Jackson Huddy will be along, and I don't want a showdown here."

She wasted no time, but when she came back Mady Coppinger was with her. "Can Mady come?" Jessica asked.

"Sure." And then he added, "Tom's with the herd."

"I've got some saddle stock out of town," Bob said, "and you'll need horses going up the trail. Leave the bay gelding with the three white stockings for me, and take the rest along."

He stepped closer and said to Tap, "Be careful. Every Munson is somewhere around." Then he went on, "You hear about Bill Taylor? He and some other fellow who was locked in the same jail, they stole the sheriff's horse and lit out. I don't think anybody minded too much, not even the sheriff. Bill proved himself pretty much of a man in this shindig."

By the time Tap had managed to get a couple of saddles and mounted the girls on the horses, it was well into the afternoon. He was growing more and more worried. Curiosity might take Huddy on into Indianola, but he would be on their trail soon, and he might be lying in wait for them somewhere to the west.

Tap wasted no time. He rode with his rifle across his saddle bows and he held to a good pace. They were leading six extra horses. All of them seemed glad to go, to be anywhere but around the storm area.

Nobody talked. Tap grew increasingly jumpy, and was ready at every sound. He changed direction again and again, trying to establish no pattern with his changes.

Around Chocolate Bay the scene was desolate. There had been a few cabins there, and some fishing boats. All these were gone. The shore was littered with debris.

At last, long after dark, he led them into camp in a corner of the Chocolate Bayou. It was on a bench above the stream, and taking a chance, he built a small fire. They made coffee and ate a little, and he prepared a place for the girls to sleep. As for himself, he drew back into the trees and bedded down in thick brush. He slept little.

At daybreak they were in the saddle once more.

16

Victoria was picking up after the storm. Tappan Duvarney had no wish to ride into the town, but they needed food, and both of the girls needed clothing.

By now Jackson Huddy would have decided where he was going, and would undoubtedly be on his trail, or perhaps be in town waiting for him.

They had seen few travelers, and most of these were going in the same direction. Everybody who could move seemed to be leaving the coast.

Not even the havoc created by the storm could rob Victoria of its quaint, Old World beauty. They came into the square, Tappan Duvarney riding warily. It was a lovely place, with roses everywhere—a charming town, but it might be a deadly one for him.

He dismounted, keeping his horse between himself and the street, which he studied with careful eyes, paying attention to the roofs, the windows, the people along the street.

"You'd best go to your folks," he said to Mady, "or

else get what you want and meet Jessica and we'll take you to Tom."

She hesitated a moment, obviously not liking the alternatives. "All right," she said.

When Mady had moved away, he spoke softly to Jessica. "I'm going to move the horses soon. They will be over in back of that building at the end of the street. Don't mention it to Mady, but if she's coming with us, you can meet me there in an hour."

When he left her he paused at the corner of a building, again studying the street. Then he went to a store, bought new clothes, and going out of the back door, took them to his horses, and led the horses off the street. He bought groceries and other supplies, always moving with caution.

He had gone into the restaurant when suddenly he saw Harry and Caddo, the two men he had seen with Mady in the buckboard that day beside the trail. He crossed to them. "Hello, Harry," he said.

The man turned and looked at him with careful eyes. "You have the advantage of me," Harry said.

"I am Tappan Duvarney. I know your name because you were with Miss Coppinger one day. I was close by, just off the trail."

Caddo grinned. "Now, I figured that. I really figured it," he said.

Harry held out his hand. "Heard about you," he said.

"Mady's in town. She's with my fiancée, Jessica Trescott. She may be riding out with us to join Tom—I'm not sure."

He heard someone coming up behind him and he turned slightly. It was Lin Stocker, who also rode for the Coppinger outfit. Duvarney remembered him with no liking.

"Jackson Huddy's huntin' you," Stocker said, with a hint of malice in his tone. "Looks like you won't be with us long."

"No. I'm going out with a trail drive."

"I didn't mean that, I meant—"

"Shut up, Stocker," Harry said shortly. "He knows what you mean . . . so do I."

Abruptly, Stocker turned and strode from the room, but when he was at the door Duvarney called after him. "Don't forget to tell them where I am, Stocker. Just don't be with them when they come hunting me."

Stocker started to speak, but he stopped, and went out.

"Most of our boys favor Tom," Harry said, "and our money is ridin' on you."

Caddo spoke suddenly, quietly. "You want help, White Man? I can use a gun."

"No . . . thanks. This is my fight."

Out of the corner of his eye he had seen Stocker start diagonally across the street. He went to the window and, standing well back, watched him cross the street and go into a saloon. In a moment he came out and started on up the street.

"If you boys will excuse me?" Tap said, and stepped out of the door.

He watched Stocker until he disappeared into another saloon further up the street, and then he came back inside the restaurant. Harry and Caddo had gone, but he found a table in a corner where he could watch the street, and ordered a meal.

It was only a few minutes later that he saw Caddo ride swiftly out of town.

"Do you mind if I join you?"

He had been so intent on watching the street that he had not noticed Jessica approaching his table.

"Mady will be along soon." She sat down in the chair he held for her, and when he was seated she asked, "Is there going to be trouble?"

"Yes."

"You would rather I was out of the way, wouldn't you?"

"Of course, but they'll wait until I come out on the street. They know where I am sitting by now, and there is no way they can come in here without exposing themselves. And you're here. So they will wait until I come outside, and I'm going to let them wait."

She searched his face. "You aren't afraid?"

He shrugged. "I expect I am, a little. Fear sets a man up sometimes for what he has to face. A little fear does no harm, just so it doesn't put a man on the run."

A man was walking across the square, a big, narrow-shouldered man with wide hips. It was Shabbit, and he was carrying a slicker wrapped around something . . . probably a rifle or a shotgun. Considering the man, it was probably the latter. He stopped on a corner just across the street that left the square alongside the restaurant. From there he could cover the door easily.

Up the street another man with the Munson look about him was leaning on a wagon wheel, smoking a cigarette.

Following his eyes, Jessica said, "You could go out the back door."

"They will have men out there, too," he said lightly.

They ate, talking only a little. He enjoyed sitting there, making them wait in the hot sun.

Suddenly the door opened and Ev Munson came in. Shabbit was with him, and another man. It was Lin Stocker.

"You comin' out?" Ev asked him. "I'm gettin' kinda tired waitin'."

"You . . . or that army it's going to take to help you?"

Ev's features flushed with anger. "I don't need no help. I never saw the day I couldn't take you, an' three like you."

Duvarney looked up at him, smiling a little. "All right, Munson, let's just talk about me. Do you want to take me? Out in the street right now?" He glanced at the others. "I mean without this carrion to help."

Stocker started to step forward, but Ev waved him back. "Sure," he taunted, "if you can get out from behind those skirts, I'll meet you outside, right now!"

Tap Duvarney got up. "Will you excuse me, Jessica?" Deliberately he raised his voice so that the three men striding to the door could hear him. "This won't take long." Under his breath he added, "Get back in the office, out of range."

He loosened his gun in its holster. He had not really thought much about a fast draw since the time he cleaned up that tough town out west, when he was sent by the army to do it, as the marshal's deputy.

He walked to the door, keeping to one side. Every Munson was out there, waiting. He had an idea Ev would hold the others off so he could make the kill himself. At the same time he knew that if he killed Every Munson they would shoot him down where he stood . . . unless he moved very quickly indeed.

Tap reached over with his left hand and turned the knob, releasing the bolt, but leaving the door almost closed. He took a short step forward, put his left hand on the door, slamming it open suddenly.

He knew what would happen. At the sudden slamming of the door Ev Munson's hair-trigger nerves would react and he would draw, and that was just what happened.

The startling slam of the opening door triggered Ev Munson's gun hand and it swept down for the six-shooter. Tap took one long step through the door and drew at the same instant. His gun muzzle came up, he saw the reckless, black-clad young man with the wolfish smile, and he fired.

The wolfish smile vanished in a sudden blotching of blood, and Tap shot again, holding the gun lower, and saw Ev Munson stagger one hesitating step forward and go on his face.

At the same instant, he switched his gun and shot at Lin Stocker, who was a few yards to the right. He shot too fast, and the bullet hit Stocker in the knee and he pitched over, losing his grip on his gun.

Tap quickly stepped back inside, jerking the door to, and wheeling, he raced up the steps. In his mind he had rehearsed every move that was to follow, and he performed them smoothly now. As he reached the top of the steps he took three long strides down the hall, grasping a chair as he left the landing, and putting it down under the trap door that led to the roof.

He stepped up on the chair, jumped, and grabbed the edge of the opening. Holding himself with one hand, he pushed back the trap, then hoisted himself through.

He took a quick step, and was under the trap to the roof itself. He released the latch, pushed open the door, and after a quick look pulled himself through to the slanting roof, where he was hidden from the street by the false front of the building. He ran along the roof, jumped to the flat roof of the next building, and went quickly to the front of it.

The man at the wagon whom he had seen earlier was standing there holding a pistol; a few feet away, Shabbit held a shotgun. Both were waiting for him to show himself. He took a careful sight along the barrel of the Smith & Wesson and shot the man by the wagon through the shoulder. He dropped the rifle and whipped sharply around.

Running to the rear of the building. Tap leaped to the roof below, then dropped into the space between the buildings. There was a door there, and he ducked through it just as a bullet smashed into the door jamb, inches from his head, stinging his face with splinters.

Instead of going out the front door, he ran across, seeing a window open, and leaped through it into the alley beyond.

At that moment there was a sudden burst of firing in the street, and he paused, gasping for breath, and puzzled. Suddenly he saw Shabbit running, and he ducked into the same narrow alley in which Duvarney stood. There was blood on Shabbit's shoulder and his face was white and frightened. He started to run, then brought up short. His shotgun started to lift, and Tap Duvarney shot him through the second button of his shirt, shot twice.

Surprised at the shooting from the street, he started

back that way, picking up the shotgun as he stepped around Shabbit. At the opening into the square, he paused, looking out.

The shooting ceased.

On the far side of the square a tall man was sitting quietly in his saddle; nearer by he saw another. Other riders were coming along both sides of the square, their guns ready. Doc Belden . . . Lawton Bean . . . Welt Spicer . . . they were all there.

He stepped out, and half a dozen guns swung to cover him until they saw who he was.

"You know somethin', Major?" Lawton Bean said, grinning at him. "Those boys weren't much on the fight. I was some surprised. Figured they'd hold up better. Why, this here shindig hardly got started until they all taken out runnin' . . . all that was able."

Doc rode up. "Are you all right?" he asked.

Tom Kittery came walking across the square. "You tryin' to hog all the fun? I almost missed out on the endin' of my own feud!"

Tappan Duvarney looked around carefully. "All right, boys," he said. "We've got some cattle waiting. Shall we get back to them?"

In his room on the second floor of the hotel Jackson Huddy held his rifle easily in his hands and looked down into the square. He could see Duvarney's shoulder . . . just a *little* more now, and . . .

"Mr. Huddy?"

He turned sharply. Jessica Trescott was standing within ten feet of him and she was holding a very steady Colt House Pistol aimed at his stomach. "Mr. Huddy, I would take it kindly if you would just put that rifle down, then unbuckle your gun belt, very carefully."

"I never shot a woman," Huddy said. "I never would."

"The reverse is not true, Mr. Huddy. This woman has never shot a man, but believe me, she certainly would. Also, I am somewhat nervous, and if I start shooting it is likely I will empty this gun into you.

"You see, Mr. Huddy, I came west to marry Mr. Duvarney. I came out here because I love him and I want to bear children for him and to live out my life with him, so if you think I am going to let a man like you come between us with a bullet, you are wrong. I will kill you, Mr. Huddy, if you do not come away from that window, get on your horse, and ride right out of our lives.

"Mady Coppinger told me you came from Alabama, Mr. Huddy. The only city in Alabama that I know is Mobile. It is very lovely at this time of year. Would you go now . . . please?"

He looked at her, and then he looked at the gun. The hand that moved was only to lift his hat. "Your pleasure, ma'am," he said, and walked from the room and down the back hall.

She followed and stood by the door, watching him ride away, sitting very straight in the saddle.

Tom Kittery stood with Tappan when she reached the street. "Mady is here," she said.

"I saw her," Tom said. "I . . . I borrowed money and loaned it to her. She's gone off to N'Orleans. I reckon I'll find somebody else, somewhere on up the trail."

"You will, Tom. I'm sure of it." Jessica turned to look up at Tap. "Come on, Tappan. Those cattle are waiting."

"And we'd better find a sky pilot," Tap commented. "We might as well make it legal while we're at it."

"Yes, that, too," she said.

"You're forgettin' somethin', Major," Spicer said. "What about Jackson Huddy?"

"Oh, don't worry about him," Jessica said. "We had a talk and he decided to go back to Alabama. If you doubt it, look in the room up over the door. You'll find his rifle and pistol there."

Tappan Duvarney looked at her quizzically. "You

know, Jessica, that's a story I would really like to hear."

"I'll tell you . . . sometime." She reached in her purse and took out the Colt. "Tappan, would you carry this for me? It is getting very heavy."

NEW FROM BANTAM AUDIO PUBLISHING
THE STORIES OF LOUIS L'AMOUR

ABOUT LOUIS L'AMOUR

"I think of myself in the oral tradition—as a troubadour, a village taleteller, the man in the shadows of the campfire. That's the way I'd like to be remembered—as a storyteller. A good storyteller."

It is doubtful that any author could be as at home in the world re-created in his novels as Louis Dearborn L'Amour. Not only could he physically fill the boots of the rugged characters he writes about, but he has literally "walked the land my characters walk." His personal experiences as well as his lifelong devotion to historical research have combined to give Mr. L'Amour the unique knowledge and understanding of the people, the events, and the challenge of the American frontier that have become the hallmarks of his popularity.

Of French-Irish descent, Mr. L'Amour can trace his own family in North America back to the early 1600s and follow their steady progression westward, "always on the frontier." As a boy growing up in Jamestown, North Dakota, he absorbed all he could about his family's frontier heritage, including the story of his great-grandfather who was scalped by Sioux warriors.

Spurred by an eager curiosity and desire to broaden his horizons, Mr. L'Amour left home at the age of fifteen and enjoyed a wide variety of jobs including seaman, lumberjack, elephant handler, skinner of dead cattle, assessment miner, and officer on tank destroyers during World War II. During his "yondering" days he also circled the world on a freighter, sailed a dhow on the Red Sea, was shipwrecked in the West Indies and stranded in the Mojave Desert. He has won fifty-one of fifty-nine fights as a professional boxer and worked as a journalist and lecturer. A voracious reader and collector of rare books, Mr. L'Amour's personal library of some 10,000 volumes covers a broad range of scholarly disciplines including many personal papers, maps, and diaries of the pioneers.

Mr. L'Amour "wanted to write almost from the time I could walk." After developing a widespread following for his many adventure stories written for the fiction magazines, Mr. L'Amour published his first full-length novel, *Hondo*, in 1953. Mr. L'Amour is now one of the four bestselling living novelists in the world. Every one of his more than 95 books are still in print and every one has sold more than one million copies. He has more million-copy bestsellers than any other living author. His books have been translated into more than a dozen languages, and more than thirty of his novels and stories have been made into feature films and television movies.

His hardcover bestsellers include *The Lonesome Gods; The Walking Drum*, his twelfth-century historical novel; *Jubal Sackett; Last of the Breed;* and *The Haunted Mesa*.

The recipient of many great honors and awards, in 1983 Mr. L'Amour became the first novelist ever to be awarded a Special National Gold Medal by the United States Congress in honor of his life's work. In 1984 he was also awarded the Medal of Freedom by President Ronald Reagan.

Mr. L'Amour lives in Los Angeles with his wife, Kathy, and their two children, Beau and Angelique.

NEW FROM BANTAM AUDIO PUBLISHING
THE STORIES OF LOUIS L'AMOUR

Now, for the first time, Louis L'Amour's bestselling stories have been dramatized for audio-cassette listening. Each 60-minute tape begins with L'Amour's newly recorded, first-hand observations and anecdotes about the *real* frontier. He then introduces an audio adaptation of a Chick Bowdrie, Texas Ranger story, complete with multi-voiced characterizations and authentic sound effects. L'Amour at his storytelling best and his fiction as you've never heard it before together on Bantam Audio Cassettes.

THE CHICK BOWDRIE SERIES